W<small>HEN</small> the gentlemen rejoined the ladies, Max used all the skill accrued in his years in the haughtiest London Salons to maneuver Daphne to a window seat. Max, his questions ready in his mind, was nonplussed when Daphne got her oar in first.

"You're the terrible Marquess! I might have known. Anyone who would indulge in such blatant blackmail must be the worst sort of person. And you hadn't even the courage to own up to your real identity!"

"Terrible? Whatever are you talking about?"

"Mama's friend, Lady Scorby, told her all about you when she visited last Spring. How you snub everybody and are terribly rude, but since you're so rich, and a peer and a bachelor, everybody pretends they like it. She also had a list of fortune hunters to beware of."

"Fortune hunters?"

"Not that she said you are one. Only that you're a heartless flirt."

Max, who had altogether different plans for this conversation, found himself laughing. He had expected Miss Daphne to be unorthodox, but she was proving an even greater diversion than he had hoped for.

Fawcett Coventry Books
by Sarah Carlisle:

CLEOPATRA'S CARPET 50009 $1.75
DAPHNE 50098 $1.75
WIDOW AUBREY 23697 $1.75

Buy them at your local bookstore or use this handy coupon for ordering.

This offer expires 5/31/81   8999

DAPHNE

a novel by

Sarah Carlisle

FAWCETT COVENTRY • NEW YORK

DAPHNE

Published by Fawcett Coventry Books, a unit of CBS Publications,
the Consumer Publishing Division of CBS Inc.

ISBN: 0-449-50098-5

Printed in the United States of America

First Fawcett Coventry Printing: September 1980

10 9 8 7 6 5 4 3 2 1

1.

John Maximillian Adolphus Wade-Hambledon was bored. Very bored. Bored with his social acquaintances, his fine houses, the round of parties and pretty little chorus dancers, his stable of horses, his title, yes, especially his title, and even with his money. Thoroughly, totally, unmitigatedly, definitively bored.

Not that this particular country manor wasn't a bit better than most. He approved of the slightly shabby plum-colored drapes his hand was fingering, the air of easy informality long rooted in country ways, the lack of pretension. In fact, he had decided previously to visit his cousin and heir, The Honorable George Wade-Hambledon, in his place in the country for the sole purpose of enjoying just such simplicity, but Wade Hall was rather too spruce for Max's taste. He had noticed the newness of the carpet laid down in the hall, the overnight disappearance of a spot he himself had left on the gray damask upholstery of the settee in the library, the absence of any dead leaves beneath the potted plants in the small conservatory, the rigid standards of the Hall's staff . . .

He was fortunate in being able to flee his kinsman's uneasy hospitality for this more casual welcome, at St. Wilfred's Close, a neighbor of George's. Now, standing as he was in the long gallery of the Close, admiring the riotous garden tucked in among the many els of the house's wings, he was regretting the necessity of leaving, dreading the return to the stiff courtesy and agitated attentions of the Hall. But his business with Sir Wilfred was at an end, a trifling matter of some blood stock settled, and reality must be faced.

As he thought about it, he nearly convinced himself that St. Wilfred's Close would probably be as bad as George's neatish property if he were to stay there long enough. The velvet drapes, their former grandeur a trifle faded by strong sunlight, a scruffy patch where the material had been pushed carelessly aside by hand after hand, would soon lose their charm.

The air wafting through the French windows was warmly laden with the sounds and smells of the garden. That curious mixture of fragrances, which has far more charm then the odor of one mere flower, the murmuring of doves in the eaves of the old buildings, the drone of a giant bumblebee, occasionally visible among the bright flowers, flooded over him and he was taken back to his childhood summers on his grandfather's country estate, where he had been allowed to forget who he was and be an ordinary little boy looking for fun and mischief. The doves became less persistent in their droning.

A flash of white drew his attention to the far side of the garden. Someone was performing a curious rite beneath the opened window sash of a room across the way. His attention stiffened as an arm, noiseless and efficient, swung up toward the open window. Something seemed to fly through the aperture into the room beyond. The white figure waited. Then the arm went into play again. Another wait. Another small projectile was sent into the room.

Max stood on tiptoe, straining his six-foot frame to provide himself with a better vantage from which to observe. A head with tousled dark blond curls came into view from behind a stand of daisies, the arm now almost invisible. Another object went through the window.

He opened the window wide and stepped through. Sir Wilfred, or his gardeners, had eschewed the fancy of graveling the surface of the path, and on the grass he gave no warning of his approach. Once around a stand of holly trees that were blocking his view, he was able to observe the mystery, now shorn of most of its secret. The hollies also gave him excellent cover, so that he was himself unobserved.

A young person, a girl in fact, was stooping under the window of what must be the music room of the mansion, if his glimpse of the harpsichord inside was any clue. The vague whisper of voices told him that the room was occupied, but whoever was there did not seem to notice the intrusion of the child's strange little gifts shooting in from the garden. The girl, who looked to be no more than fourteen, clasped a small box in her left hand, to which she repaired whenever new ammunition was required. An occasional squeaky, scrabbling sound heightened the sense of mystery.

Another offering was sent on its way.

Max waited for the girl's next move. This pause seemed longer than the earlier ones. Was she to continue this senseless pantomime? Had she revealed herself to the unseen occupants of the room? Why did she comport herself with such secrecy and stealth? And above all, what in the world was this all about?

A shake of the box told him one thing. It had apparently surrendered its last, its last . . . its last whatever it was she was throwing. What in the world could it be? Damn!

The curly head lifted cautiously to the sill of the window, sufficient to allow the child a view of the room, but no more. Max wondered with amazement that the people inside were sufficiently engrossed in their conversation to have remained in ignorance of the whole situation. Whatever was being thrown at them, it seemed not to have attracted their attention. Looking closer, he saw quite clearly a pout of disgust on the child's face.

Or perhaps she wasn't quite a child. Now that he could examine her at his leisure, he saw that he must revise his estimate of her age. True, the schoolroom dress was in keeping with his first impression of extreme youth, as was the general air of childish practical jokes that surrounded the incident. But it was an outfit of fine muslin, slightly soiled, trimmed with bright blue silk ribbons and a row of lace at the hem. It was the dress of a young lady, or at least of a girl of gentle birth. This was no gardener's child bent on mischief.

The sunlight played over her hair, highlighting the shots of true gold that wove through its tawny splendor. Eyes that were dark blue without a hint of paleness glimmered under long sable lashes. The figure showed unmistakable signs of maturity, the mouth had a lilt to it that spoke of self-possession.

The hair, with its magnificent color and abundance, reminded him of the portrait in the grand hall of the present baronet's lady on the occasion of her wedding. Perhaps this was a daughter, a younger child just on the verge of leaving the schoolroom. He had a vague recollection of an elder daughter to be shot off in the coming Season, but this girl seemed too young to be her. The rumor he had heard was that a series of family disasters had postponed that elder girl's presentation to Society for the whole of three Seasons, making her a bit long in the tooth to be mistaken for this minx.

So, a younger daughter, caught in the midst of some prank. Childish and rather amusing, an incident that brought back memories of his own youthful mischief. He stopped to analyze his data, then smiled to himself as he reshaped his conclusions. A younger daughter of Sir Wilfred's, perhaps encouraged to keep her childish ways until her older sister was happily settled. The theory fit neatly. For, from what he could see, this child had the sort of looks that would give the other young lady unwanted competition on the marriage mart. It was wise of the parents to dispose of one daughter before releasing this imp on Society. She'd turn many a head.

But time was passing. In all likelihood, his host would soon return with the papers he had set off in search of, and Sir Wilfred would be wondering where Max had gone to. And Cousin George would be donning his oh, so proper gloves, adjusting his modish hat to a nicety, as he courteously refrained from wondering aloud at his relative's dilatory habits.

The girl had begun to creep away from the house, making her way with caution through the herbaceous border she had trampled into for a more convenient post beneath the window. Max saw that the promise he had glimpsed was more than fulfilled. A beautiful face with small, straight nose and curving mouth, framed by that mane of hair, a rounded figure and above-average height carried by graceful carriage, but above all, that indefinable élan of poise and expression that marked the beginning of a natural style, all were there. On an impulse, he allowed her to walk some distance from the open window, and its listeners inside, before he stepped forward to accost her. For speak he must. Too many questions teased his brain to allow him to let the opportunity of having them answered slip away.

"Good afternoon."

It was a commonplace greeting, one he wished he could improve on, but he was willing to make do with it in a pinch. It did not explain the girl's guilty start and the noisy gasp she made as she spun around to face him, eyes wide with panic. So she did have a conscience. Or perhaps Sir Wilfred was a strict parent, despite the appearance of easygoing ways.

"Who are you?"

He thought for a moment, then smiled. "My name is Max Wade-Hambledon. And whom might you be?"

"Wade-Hambledon? Oh, no! You must be another relative of George's."

He caught himself smiling at the sound of dismay in her voice. "Is that so bad?"

"Bad? No, not a bit, but it is a trifle awkward. Have you been in the garden for some time?"

"Perhaps. But you have yet to tell me your name."

This brought her back to some realization of her duties of courtesy, and she executed a hasty curtsy and murmured apologetically, "I'm Daphy, I mean Daphne St. Wilfred. Do forgive me, but I was so busy—I mean, I was so surprised when you appeared like this—I mean, I had no idea . . . And you would be a relative!" She cast an anxious glance back at the window. "I say, you won't give me away, will you?"

"Give you away?"

"Then you must not have seen . . . Thank you so much, so very much, I'm sure, if you will just excuse me now, Mama and Miss Singleton will be looking for me, I'm sure. I must go present myself." Her relief was palpable.

11

He arrested her flight with a cautionary hand. "You are altogether too quick to jump to conclusions. Perhaps I did see something."

"Oh, dear."

"And I'm not above a spot of blackmail, either, young Miss Daphne."

"Blackmail?" The word seemed to bewilder more than alarm her. "Oh, please don't tell Mama, she would never understand!"

"I won't, provided you answer one or two little questions for me."

Despite her anxiety, she greeted this request with caution. "Whatever can I tell you? I'm sure you can't be interested in anything I know. Miss Singleton says that I don't know much of anything at all." She smiled with such guileless innocence that he almost laughed aloud.

"But there are one or two things that only you can tell me."

"Oh, surely not!" She sidled toward the path.

"We shall see. For example, whatever were you taking from your box and tossing through the window?"

With a sudden giggle, she glanced down at the box still in her hand. The eyes that rose to meet his were alight with mischief. "Why, it was but a collection of small things, of no importance, sir."

"But nonetheless, you must appreciate my curiosity."

By now she was grinning. "Very well, sir, I *shall* assuage it. My box was full of mice."

He would never have imagined such an answer to his question and could not help doubting he had heard right. "Mice?"

"Mice."

2.

She turned as if to leave, the mischievous grin on her face showing that she was more than satisfied with his reaction to her oh, so simple answer. But her explanation was *too* simple for his tastes, and he grabbed her roughly by the arm and dragged her to a bower formed by the overhanging branches of the peach and cherry trees that grew on the other side of the brick wall. He pushed her onto the stone seat, having cleared a space for her among the branches. The bees active in this end of the garden refused to let so minor an event disturb them, and the conversation was carried out to their lazy, moaning accompaniment.

"Young ladies don't play with mice, Miss Daphy, I mean, Miss Daphne!"

"I don't want to be a young lady."

15

"Well, perhaps you are but a schoolgirl, but still . . ."

"Mama and Papa say that I'm not that, either. At least, Papa says that it's high time—" He interrupted her with an impatient wave of his hand.

"Now, what is this all about?"

The grin played once again on her lips. "I mustn't tell." It was obvious to him that she had somehow lost her fear of him.

"If you don't, I shall tell your papa!"

"Oh, no, you wouldn't! That would be ungentlemanly and disloyal of you." She was sure of her reasoning, but indignant at his callow sham.

He produced his most forbidding scowl, the one reserved for intimidating only the most recalcitrant of his retainers.

"Oh, please, I meant no harm. It was for their sake—George and Emily's."

The scowl was replaced by an uplifted eyebrow. "That tells me nothing."

"Oh, well, I suppose I must tell you *everything*, in that case. But only if you promise not to breathe a word of this to anyone! I was not enjoying idle mischief, I assure you. In fact, my motives are of the noblest."

A look of amused doubt entered his eyes, but he nodded his agreement. "But I must warn you that this promise is conditional. I'll reserve the right to judge the case if your tale is not a convincing one."

"It's all for the sake of Emily and George," she repeated in a rush, not heeding his words.

"By George I assume you mean my cousin, George Wade-Hambledon. But who is Emily?"

"Why, my sister is Emily, of course. She is some four years older than I."

"I wonder that I've never met her."

"That's just the problem. And she and George were finally together, alone, in the music room, after I had tried so hard to get them there, and this was my very first chance to help them along a bit, so you see, my intentions are really of the purest. I really could not let such an opportunity slip through my fingers," she ended wistfully.

"My dear young lady, I understand nothing at all. Do start at the beginning. All of this seems nonsensical at best."

"But the beginning was Great-aunt Emily—that's Emmie's godmother and namesake, you understand—and as I was saying, the beginning was with her falling so dreadfully ill that we despaired for her life three years ago, and she insisted on having Emmy at her bedside throughout—"

"Wait, wait! I'm understanding even less. Nothing at all. Perhaps you should answer my questions. If only I can guess what to ask."

"Certainly." She arranged the white muslin gown, charming despite its innocence of allure, into demure folds on the bench, and waited, a polite expression on her face. She reminded him of a well-mannered schoolboy being asked to recite by his master, awaiting the cue to trot out his hard-won hoard of knowledge. Despite himself, he felt the first overwhelming swells of laughter rising in him, and he firmly pushed them away.

"For some reason it is important that George and Emily are together, alone, in the music room."

"It really doesn't matter which room, you see—"

He sternly shushed her. "Now, this seems highly improper, I must say, and I'm surprised that any well-regulated family would allow such a thing to happen, but if it is so, it is so."

"I'm supposed to be with them, or at least in the vicinity, but it is all so innocent between them, and George is really the epitome of respectability—in fact, rather a dull dog—that Mama wouldn't mind if she knew that I had wandered into the garden. She would understand, in any case. They are discussing nothing but music, which I find excessively dull, you see. They never seem to be interested in any of the gay tunes I sometimes hear Papa's hunting guests sing after dinner."

"I can imagine." And Max could well guess at what some of Sir Wilfred's cronies would sing after an evening at board, passing the port amongst themselves, and the image of his prim cousin George singing such songs was so out of the realm of possibility that the laughter within him began to win over decorum. "What is the significance of this tête-à-tête? If they are but discussing music—"

"I want them to discuss more than that. I was only trying to give them an opportunity, you see," she explained, eagerness lighting her face.

18

"But why?"

"It's so simple! They're to make a match of it." Her pleasure was so palpable, as she made this outrageous explanation, that he almost felt compelled to hurry to the music room and congratulate the young couple on their good fortune.

"My dear child—I mean Miss Daphne—I believe that my cousin would have informed me of such a state of affairs, if that were the case."

"Oh, they don't know it yet."

His mind began to spin before the onslaught of her unbelievable statements, each presented with such an air of candor and assurance that he suspected that there was something she had not yet told him. Or perhaps he had missed some vital point in his confusion.

She interrupted his thoughts with alarming nonchalance. "Of course."

"Of course." It would appear that Miss Daphne's imagination had slipped the restraints of reality, but Max refused to be daunted. In fact, he thought he was beginning to enjoy this wild adventure even more. Whatever she was up to, it seemed harmless enough, and he did not recall having a similiar conversation with a young lady of birth and breeding at any time in his career. Then the memory of the carefully-aimed missiles, those mice, intruded on his thoughts.

"Whatever have the mice to do with it? I didn't think that young ladies would touch such things. Shouldn't you have fainted at the sight of one?"

"Exactly! You do understand, after all."

19

"But I understand nothing!" he protested. "Aren't you afraid of mice?"

"No. But Emily is."

He was tempted to follow this alluring sidepath, but her possession of the mice still teased him. "Where did you get them?"

"From Sym in the stables. He trapped them for me."

"Is that a part of his normal duties?"

"Oh, no—it was all a secret, of course. I paid him a penny a head for them. That was what he insisted they're worth. I'd never bought mice before, so I really couldn't be sure if it was a fair price."

"I'm relieved that you haven't made a career of tossing mice into windows."

"It was only for an emergency, you see. I had it all planned, after George's last visit, when they went into the music room to look at some sheet music, and I had Sym save me a whole boxful. You don't think I paid too much, do you?"

"I can't say. I'm not familiar with the current market price of field mice."

"I used the last of my pin-money on them. I shall have to borrow from Emily again."

He sighed. "So we have George and Emily in the music room."

"Yes. But it is all blameless."

"Quite."

"Such a pity, too. I've been working on them so hard, for months, ever since Papa announced his decision, but they don't seem to realize ..." Her voice trailed off, but he was beginning to have a glimmer of understanding of her motives. He tried again.

"You're trying to arrange a friendship between your sister Emily and my cousin George. In fact, you think that they should marry!"

"Yes, I do. Don't you think it an excellent scheme?"

"What I think has little to do with it. It's in the hands of George and your papa."

"And Emily."

"And Emily," he agreed absentmindedly. "You're too young to interfere in this way."

"I can't believe that you would say such a mean-spirited thing! No one else is bothering, and it's of the greatest importance, and someone must help them!"

He fell back before her vehemence. "Perhaps, but you're still too young. And I don't understand the need for urgency. Why not let nature take its course?"

"But I told you! First Great-aunt Emily was ill, then Grandpapa Mountjoy died, then Emily herself, silly widgeon, suffered that nasty fall from her mare, although how she could have allowed such a thing to happen, I don't know. Her little pony is the sweetest thing imaginable, and besides, she lacks the energy to swish her tail at flies, much less throw anyone. It must have been something silly Emily did. She's not a great horsewoman."

Max fought against the confusion that this jumble of confidences brought with it, and he stuck manfully to the salient facts.

"But why can't you leave it to George and Emily, and perhaps your mama and papa, which would be more seemly, to arrange for the match? You're not yet out of the schoolroom."

"But I will be!" Her anguish was real, but he didn't know what to say in the face of it, or how to say it. Instead, his practical mind moved on to the other questions that had teased him from the first moment he had seen Daphne's strange conduct.

"But why? Can you tell me why?"

"They ought to get married, that's why!"

"No, no, I'm not asking about that. At least, not yet. What I want to know is, why did you throw all those mice through the window?"

Before she could give him the answer he so craved, a series of short, shrill screams penetrated the peaceful, sun-filled air of the garden, jabbing both of them so that they rose to their feet.

Daphne's face lit up with a pleased smile. "There! It's worked after all. I told you so."

She ran toward the music room, Max following on her heels.

3.

St. Wilfred's Close had once been the grounds of a cloistered monastery housing a contemplative order of monks. One wing of the present building, that which held the kitchen offices, still-rooms, and buttery, with their attached garden, was all that remained of the religious buildings, although much of the architecture of the Close still carried a faint ecclesiastical air. There were still reminders of what the place had once been scattered around the grounds and countryside, and the old sundial that had counted the monks' time for them graced the kitchen garden. In fact, the plan of that garden followed the one first laid out by some distant monk in the twelfth century, the herb beds still occupied as they once had been when, according to the records still treasured on the estate, the order had first taken possession of the property.

Unlike many such religious houses in England, St. Wilfred's had not died a violent death. The bells had rung the offices undisturbed, calling the faithful to worship, the monks had scurried through the halls, rosaries swinging at their sides, wayfarers had sought and found shelter. But there had been fewer and fewer monks to answer the bells. Then, one terrible year near the end of the fifteenth century, the sweating sickness had left the monastery with very few occupants indeed, a mere half-dozen of the monks surviving.

And so it was that, well before the upheaval of the Reformation and King Henry's confused marriages, the few remaining monks, led by their noble young abbot, had left their home for the shelter of a larger and more prosperous house nearby. Their way was paid by a local landowner, who generously endowed the welcoming establishment, and everyone was happy with the new arrangement. St. Wilfred's dissolved without a murmur of protest.

It seemed only right and proper that the generous neighbor, who had seen to the monks' provision, should receive from the hands of the abbot the monastic building of St. Wilfred's and the considerable acreage attached. That the abbot was the second son of the neighbor went uncommented. A new order had begun.

Sir Wilfred St. Wilfred was the eleventh baronet to inherit that order. A happy, prosperous man, he failed to impress the observer with his stature or visage. In fact, he was round and tubby with a florid, pouty face bewhiskered at lip and cheek, but a kinder husband, a gentler father, a better landlord could not be found. In the bosom of his family, standing beside his statuesque wife and daughters, with even young Willie, the baby of the family, a full head taller than he, he looked slightly ridiculous. But a closer acquaintanceship revealed a natural dignity and simple wisdom that were admirable. Sir Wilfred loved his family, his land, and his horses, in that order, and he abhorred the stir and bustle he held were the curses of urban dwelling.

It was some thirty minutes before peace was restored to St. Wilfred's Close after the household had been summoned to Miss St. Wilfred's side by that young lady's screams. This daughter, while entertaining her family's nearest neighbor, The Hon. George Wade-Hambledon, had had the frightening experience of observing a small, gray field mouse making its way in a confused manner across the Turkish carpet that covered the floor of her mother's music room. Upon suffering this shock to her tender sensibilities, she had screamed loudly and repeatedly, then slumped into a faint.

It was only the presence of George Wade-Hambledon that had prevented the disaster of her falling to the floor in her unconscious state, leading to a possible injury. He had manfully stepped forward and caught her in his arms, then carried her to the nearby sofa. His gentle murmurs and assurances that all was well did little to stir Miss St. Wilfred back to life, and he was nervously chafing her wrists, under the supervision of a surprisingly inactive Miss Daphne St. Wilfred,

25

when the whole of the household descended from all parts of the building, even the stables, to fill the small, pleasant room. The scene that met their eyes was a touching one, of the sort beloved of lady novelists. A kneeling George tenderly ministered to the fallen angel.

Unfortunately, only Daphne appreciated it.

"Whatever have you done?" Lady St. Wilfred demanded, her full bosom heaving with emotion and exertion as she glared at George. The heat of the day and the unusual effort she had made in hurrying to her daughter's side had caused a bead of sweat to build on the tip of her aristocratic nose. In her excitement and confusion, she spoke rather more sharply than courtesy dictated.

"I am not sure, m'lady," the rescuer stuttered. "Something has caused Miss St. Wilfred to faint."

The young lady's brother spotted the reason for the crisis while everyone else still clustered about the victim. "There's a mouse in here." He pointed toward the French window, through which a small, gray animal was fleeing, but only his other sister, Daphne, seemed to be paying him any heed.

"Shhh!" she hissed, hurrying over to pinch his arm.

"In fact, there are two mice," a lazy voice remarked from the door to the hall. This comment drew considerably more notice, or rather its speaker did.

"Cousin Edenbury!" George Wade-Hambledon said from his position at the young lady's side. He appeared to be struggling to his feet, despite the encumbrance of an unconscious figure still in his arms.

26

"Please don't disturb yourself, George," Max answered. "If you do, you can't help but disturb Miss St. Wilfred."

By speaking, he drew the attention of his host. "My Lord Edenbury! There you are. Can't think where you got off to," Sir Wilfred exclaimed. Being free of his daughter's reclining figure, he had no trouble attaining his feet. "Some freak has caused poor Emmie here to faint dead away. Can't think what it could have been."

"Nor can I," George added. "One minute we were poring over a Mozart minuet, the next she was screaming her head . . . I mean, she was showing every sign of considerable distress."

"Perhaps Mozart was distasteful to her," his cousin murmured.

"What? Surely not. You jest, cousin." The younger man's discomfort, instead of raising qualms of conscience in his cousin's breast, as should have been the case, merely stirred some imp of mischief.

"Then perhaps it was something you said or did, George. Now, I wonder. What could it have been?" He considered the flushed face of the kneeling man with careful attention, as though his expression would reveal the answer to this question. It's very difficult to look imposing on one's knees.

"It wasn't old George at all," young Willie put in. "It was a mouse."

"Mouse? Nonsense," his father sputtered. "No mouse, I mean, mice in this house. The stables, now . . ."

"Are surely a far more suitable habitat for mice," his senior guest agreed. "But I fear that your son is right, Sir Wilfred. I, too, saw such a creature make its escape through the French window."

"See? No one ever listens to me," Willie interjected. His papa shushed him, but there was no need. Max had paid the boy not the slightest heed.

"In fact, I saw not one mouse, nor even a mere two, but rather a whole family of them. I wonder how one should refer to such a multitude of mice? Does one call them a herd?"

"Why not a flock?" Miss Daphne retorted.

"A litter?" suggested Sir Wilfred.

Max shook his head. "I misled you when I said they were a family. They all seemed to be quite adult. Not a baby amongst them."

"It could be a pride, like a pride of lions!" Willie said.

"Oh, really!" from his sister.

"Yes, pride. I like that. A pride of mice. Now, I wonder how a pride of mice managed to find their way, all together, into Lady St. Wilfred's music room. Curious, isn't it?"

He was staring thoughtfully at Daphne's crimson face, but fortunately for that young lady, all attention was once again focused on the recumbent figure on the sofa. Miss Emily St. Wilfred was regaining consciousness.

"Dearest Emmie, are you all right?" her mother asked anxiously.

"I'm not sure, Mama. I can't remember what happened."

"You have fainted, Miss St. Wilfred," George Wade-

Hambledon said with every sign of tender concern.

Emily, looking up to see that she was still in the arms of a man other than her father, brother or clergyman, looked as if she were going to faint again.

"None of that!" her father ordered. He seized the vinaigrette his wife had been holding ineffectually and waved it vigorously under the girl's nose. "There. Now, don't be silly."

"You must lie back on the cushion, Emmy, dear," Lady St. Wilfred urged. Emily, still blushing, merely nodded her agreement, and, with the assistance of her mother and George, made herself comfortable against the satin of the sofa. An imposing figure in black silk, the keys of her office rattling at her waist, began to fan her face with vigor.

"There, there, miss. I am sure that it will all be fine." Miss Fernwick, incensed by the insults her housekeeping had drawn from young master Wilfred and the tall stranger lounging against the mantel, turned to do battle where she could.

"Master Wilfred, I am sure that there was no such thing as a mouse in this room. You must have imagined that you saw such a thing. There can be no other explanation."

Willie opened his mouth to protest, turning to Max for support, but a wink from that quarter soothed his indignation. For perhaps the first time in his life, tact seemed the reasonable course to take when dealing with his mother's housekeeper. Engaging in an unseemly squabble in the presence of a Whip, of a gentleman who owned the smashing team that had pulled old George up the drive to the Close, was unthinkable.

"Yes, ma'am," he murmured as he sidled toward the fireplace. Without realizing it, he had learned a valuable lesson, and all for the hope of riding behind the grays.

Miss Fernwick, surprised and mollified by this easy capitulation, was left with her ready retort, already framed for his expected insolence, on the tip of her tongue, and unusable.

"Miss Fernwick, perhaps a sip of port wine will revive poor Emily more completely," Lady St. Wilfred said from her place by the sofa. "Will you be so good as to have some fetched?"

"But of course, Lady St. Wilfred. And I shall disperse that unseemly congregation of servants now crowding the hall. I can't imagine what Margold can be thinking, to allow them to hang about like a band of holiday makers at the fair."

With this less than tactful comment, aimed at her archrival, the butler, she sailed from the room, her skirts billowing out behind her.

"Please, Mama, I'm quite fine now," Emily protested as she struggled to sit up. She was now free of George's support, but the housekeeper had made her keenly aware of the spectacle she had created.

"Miss St. Wilfred, you must not exert yourself," George urged, placing a restraining hand on her arm.

Lady St. Wilfred gave him her support. "That is quite right. Whatever startled you, it is obvious that it was sufficient to induce the most violent reaction. You must rest and allow your head to clear."

"Please, pay heed to your mother, dear Miss St. Wilfred. She knows what is best for you," George added.

Emily, touched and confused by this show of attention from the young man, blushed and cast down her eyes. "I can't think what it could have been that caused me to faint like that. You must not think that I am vaporish as a rule, Mr. Wade-Hambledon. I'm not, truly. There is only one thing that has ever caused me to faint merely from the sight of it . . ."

Here she stopped, a stricken look on her face, for Miss Fernwick had re-entered the room, bearing in her own hands a tray that supported a decanter of port wine and a crystal goblet.

"I have brought the wine, as you asked, m'lady. I thought it best to see to it myself. That crowd of ruffians in the hall was quite incapable . . ."

"Thank you, Miss Fernwick," her mistress said, her voice loud enough to drown out the last of the housekeeper's complaint. "If you would be so kind as to place it on this table, and then perhaps pour Miss Emily a small portion of it . . ." Her voice trailed off, for the housekeeper had again seized the initiative and the task was already performed.

"I am sure that Miss St. Wilfred will find a taste of port soothing and strengthening, m'lady," the servant said with just a hint of emphasis on her more formal use of the precise style of the young lady's name.

"There, Emily, that will do you right," Sir Wilfred said in his heartest tone, the one he used on his sick horses and hounds. "Just the thing." He snatched the goblet from Miss Fernwick's hand and gave it to his daughter, glaring at her until she had sipped some of the wine, a dutiful smile on her face.

"What's it taste like?" Daphne asked.

"It's a bit sticky . . ."

"Daphne, how could you tease your sister like that? And you have interrupted your father, too," her mother scolded.

"But I have never been allowed to taste strong wine, and I wanted to know!"

Sir Wilfred came to her rescue. "There, there, Margaret, she meant no harm. Much better to treat the whole incident lightly, now that it's over. No harm came of it."

"No harm! Emmie might have struck her head on the furniture, or broken a bone when she fell to the floor. Or even suffered a bruise on her face . . . !"

"She could have gotten a black eye, that would have been fun," Willie piped in. "That's what happened to Sym in the stable. He was chasing after mice one day, just yesterday afternoon, in fact, although I can't understand why he should want . . ."

A vicious pinch on the arm, administered by his sister, silenced him.

"Mice, that's the only thing that's ever made Emmie faint like that," Sir Wilfred said casually. "Can't think how it is, but it's a fact, Edenbury. Curious, what?" He had long since retreated to the mantelpiece, and from there was unaware of his wife's warning glance.

"Most curious," his guest agreed.

"We have so much to thank Mr. Wade-Hambledon

for, don't we, Emmie dear? It was he who saved you from some frightful injury," Lady St. Wilfred said loudly, hoping to cover the gentlemen's comments, in particular the unfortunate reference to mice. Happily, Miss Fernwick was more tolerant of the baronet's vagaries than she was of his son's. And Max was far too imposing a figure for her to even consider taking offense at his ready support of the mouse theory.

"Oh, well, have to expect this sort of thing in the country, you know. Not that I mind such a small thing as mice. Would put up with far worse just for the fresh air and riding. You should visit here in the fall, Edenbury. Fine hunting country we have hereabouts. Not that it matches up to the Quorn, of course, but fine nonetheless. We had some fine runs last year, fine runs. There's a particularly large breed of fox that inhabits the fields over by Pippin's Ford. Excellent sport. Excellent."

"Yes, the minor inconvenience of a pride of mice in the music room is nothing compared to the joys of country life," his guest agreed with a humorous glance at the second daughter of the house.

But the baronet was off on his favorite topic. The group in the music room slowly dispersed to the sound of hunting tales: Emmie to her room with Lady St. Wilfred and an unwilling Daphne in attendance, Willie to the stable to investigate the mystery of Sym's interest in mice, and Miss Fernwick to her office below-stairs. George hovered in the hall, uncertain of where he belonged, until Daphne suddenly decided that her sister was far too great a burden for her and her mother to support on the stairs without masculine assistance. Would Mr. Wade-Hambledon be so kind...?

Ignoring his family, including the victim of one of the hazards of country life, Sir Wilfred led his chief guest back to the masculine sanctum of the estate's office, there to pore over maps of the neighborhood, explaining the best courses and the worst pitfalls, Max murmuring appropriate comments as the need arose.

In the course of the conversation, an invitation that had been heretofore declined was renewed, and, on the pretext of continuing the hunting talk, accepted. The possible wishes of George were ruthlessly ignored, sartorial considerations thrust aside, the cousins were to stay to dine. Max was still driven by curiosity over the pride of mice, and the only suitable confidant for this was Miss Daphy, the one person who knew all. He still had many questions to put to that young lady.

4.

Max sat through the dinner in the restless grip of impatience. Dish followed dish, course followed interminable course. It was the longest dinner he had ever endured, and he had to force himself at times to eat, to drink, to say all that was proper.

Which is not to say that it wasn't a fine meal. The food, its country freshness enhanced by skillful preparation, was enough to entice even a jaded palate. The wines that accompanied the meal were the finest, the service impeccable. And the conversation that flew around him showed how lively and complex was the family he had sat down with.

"Do you know about the discovery of Ceres, sir?" Willie asked.

Max turned to him with surprise. "Ceres? I didn't know she had been rediscovered."

"Willie, how could you?" this from his mother.

"It ain't the classical one he's talking about," began his father.

"More's the pity," George added in a tone suitable for the pulpit.

Max laughed at Willie. "I gather you don't mean the goddess of grain? For a moment I wondered if your thoughts had turned to agriculture, although why they should be in Latin, I didn't understand. What is it you speak of?"

"It's that dreadful astrology!"

"It ain't astrology, it's astronomy! An Italian named Piazzi discovered it but a few years ago. Surely you've heard of it, sir, coming from London as you do."

"Willie, this is not the sort of conversation that is suitable for the table," Emily said.

"Nor is it suitable for a gentleman! Astrology! Why, it is very like witchcraft." Lady St. Wilfred stabbed at her tart with angry energy.

"It is not, it's a science. Men like Mr. Herschel and Mr. Haley, and Sir Isaac Newton, they are all scientists. . . ."

"Mr. Herschel? The name sounds foreign to me," George countered.

"What difference does that make? He lived in England when he . . ."

"And this Piazza fellow, he sounds Italian," added his father.

"Piazzi, Papa. His name is Piazzi. According to a tract Willie has, he has discovered something called an asteroid. I think I have it right, don't I, Willie?" Daphne turned to her brother for confirmation.

"This is not a fitting subject for a young lady to show interest in," their mother intervened, flustered.

"Why not?"

"Astrology . . ."

"Is different from astronomy," Sir Wilfred said triumphantly, as if he had been supporting his son all along.

"Exactly," that youngster said with satisfaction.

"Precisely," agreed Daphne.

"It is still no fitting topic for discussion at *my* table."

A small silence fell after Lady St. Wilfred's pronouncement. Max found that he was staring at Daphne, his curiosity rekindled. First mice, now the stars. . . .

Sir Wilfred's comment broke into his thoughts. "And it is not the sort of work or interest suitable for a country gentleman."

"I *will* study it, I *will*! I shall devote the rest of my life to it!"

"That's what you said about the navy," Emily commented in a matter-of-fact way.

"You were going to be a sailor, then captain of your own ship, and finally admiral of the fleet, until you visited Uncle Mountjoy on the *Euterpe*. That cured you fast enough." Daphne's tone was as crushing as her sister's.

"Midshipman!" Willie started to explain. "Not sailor! Mid . . ."

His sisters ignored him.

"The dreadful smell!" Emily said with feeling.

"And the crowding!" Daphne agreed.

"And all those hammocks rocking with the motion of the waves. Quite enough to turn anyone's stomach," Sir Wilfred said, shaking his head with the memory. He cast a commiserating glance at his son, then turned to listen to his guest.

"Fortunate, perhaps," Max murmured.

"Most fortunate. He's the last of the line. Can't let the name die. Dare say I should take a firmer line with him, whip him into shape. Some things ain't befitting his birth." Here the old gentleman leaned back to pat his tummy, and Max knew that Willie was in no danger of harsh treatment from his papa. This was not the case when neighbor George was concerned. That worthy was taking a deep breath as if preparatory to the delivery of another sermon.

Sir Wilfred waved his hand, the wine was returned to the sideboard, and Lady St. Wilfred was on her feet. George was left to bow politely to the departing ladies.

When the gentlemen rejoined the ladies, Max used all the skill accrued in years in the haughtiest London salons and maneuvered Daphne to a window seat in the drawing room where they all had gathered. From there they could overlook the garden, scene of their first encounter.

Max, his questions ready in his mind, was nonplussed when Daphne got her oar in first.

"You're the terrible marquess! I might have known. Anyone who would indulge in such blatant blackmail

38

must be the worst sort of person. And you hadn't even the courage to own up to your real identity!"

"Terrible? Whatever are you talking about?" He was surprised, for this onslaught, the last thing he had expected, also raised the question of just why he *had* failed to identify himself fully.

"Mama's friend, Lady Scorby, told her all about you when she visited last spring. How you snub everybody and are terribly rude, but since you're so rich, and a peer and a bachelor, everyone pretends they like it."

Something inside Lord Edenbury twisted sharply. "Whatever can you mean?"

Daphne's severity increased. "You snubbed someone called Miss Mapleton quite severely, after flirting with her for the whole of a fortnight."

He couldn't deny this. "And how do you know such things? Surely your mama and this Lady Scorby didn't repeat such tales in your presence."

"No. They didn't know that I was listening."

"Then it is you who deserve to be chastised, and not me. A lady does not eavesdrop. You have no right to criticize my conduct."

She thought a moment. "No, I suppose I don't. But you do have a reputation. Lady Scorby was warning Mama about you, for Emily's sake this Season, you know. She also had a list of fortune hunters to beware of."

"Fortune hunters?"

"Not that she said you are one. Only that you're a heartless flirt. She said you're quite rich." Seeing that this had failed to placate him, she added, "And I must

39

say, that Miss Mapleton sounded rather a silly creature. Perhaps she deserved a snub."

His lordship's face, which had worn all the disagree-
ableness about a haughty mouth and cold eye that
was so feared by London Society, softened into a smile.
"But that still gave me no leave to forget my manners."

"No, it didn't. But one can't always do the right
thing."

Max, who had had altogether different plans for
this conversation, found himself laughing.

"It's also unusual for a young lady to toss mice into
a room, for the apparent purpose of causing her elder
sister to faint into a young man's arms. That was
remarkably bad *ton*, you know."

"Yes, and ill-bred and rag-mannered, and all sorts
of other things."

"It doesn't seem to be bothering you."

"No, not at all."

"Why did you do it? I suspect that your sister and
my cousin will be reaching an agreement without any
help from you. Why bother?"

"I know they will make a match of it eventually, or
I should never have decided to embark on this scheme.
But you see, they are so slow about it!"

"What difference does that make?"

She stared at him, aghast. "We shall be moving to
London in only a little time. Mama says so. They
must be engaged beforehand, or it will be a miserable
time for us all."

He chuckled at her insistence. "My silly, dearest

40

widgeon, the purpose of a London Season is to allow the young lady to find a husband. If she is to become engaged before arriving there, there would be no point to it all. No one would bother."

"Certainly not, if they are all like Papa. He dislikes the notion of leaving the country excessively. But she will most surely be unhappy if she is not attached before we get there."

"Why?"

To his surprise, she was blushing. "Because I shall be there, too." Seeing his raised eyebrows, she rushed on. "I thought you understood. Papa has decided that I am old enough to be shot off now, to save the fuss of doing it all over again next year. You see, because of Great-aunt Emily and all those other things I told you about, Emily's presentation was delayed for three years. I am four years younger than she, but Papa thinks nothing of sending both of us to town in the same year. He says that my being a bit young won't hurt at all."

He was still staring at her, a thoughtful frown furrowing the skin between his fine dark brows. A glance in Emily's direction, sitting beside her father and mother on a scarlet sofa in the dim light from the fire, made clear what he was thinking. The brilliance of the silk upholstery framing her did little more than show up the paleness of Emily's coloring and looks. She was pretty enough, with soft fair hair and regular features, but she lacked the sparkle and vitality of her younger sister. Any comparison between the two of them would always leave Emily the lesser. Daphne caught his glance and blushed even more furiously.

"You see, she says that we will be the youngest and oldest debutantes in Society, so that everyone will laugh at us for that. I will not be seventeen until November."

Max smiled at her, a quick, reassuring look that promised he would keep her secret. Taking courage, she leaned closer and whispered, "There is more, although I haven't said this to Emily. You see, I have a far larger dowry than she."

She made this sound like a confession to the darkest of sins, rather than an advantage that would increase her attraction in the worldly and materialistic aristocracy that made up the *haut monde* of English Society. "And so perhaps the list of fortune hunters was drawn up for your protection, not your sister's?"

"Yes. You do understand, don't you? My godmother left me some money, I don't know quite precisely how much, and a property in London. In fact, we will be staying in the town house I inherited while we're there. It's all so very awkward."

"Emily will feel embarrassed by her age, something she can bear no blame for, but it will tell against her as she stands among younger girls in their first Season. Your presence will serve to underscore it all."

Daphne nodded her head, a miserable look on her face that touched Max's sympathy. "She is very sensitive."

"And it is to be expected that you will be the more sought after of the two, for you will have the added allure of a brilliant dowry, something that no one can

42

overlook when your family is housed in a home owned by you and not your father."

"I wish he had consented to renting one, but I suppose it would be silly, for Godmother's house is quite comfortable and very fashionably situated. Lady Scorby said that we would be quite foolish not to use it."

"I fancy that Mrs. Giles Roehampton was your godmother. Am I right?"

"Yes. Then you have heard of her!"

"Her home was a mecca for civilized entertainment for twenty years. It is lovely in itself, and the associations it bears will undoubtedly do much to lend prestige to you and your family."

"But it will make poor Emily feel so, so . . ."

"So like a poor relative, living on your bounty."

"Oh, dear, it can't be as bad as that!"

He paused a moment, considering how frank he should be with her. "On the tongues of Society's so-called wits, it could be far worse." A heavy silence fell while he considered what he had learned.

It was unbelievably naive of Sir Wilfred to insist that both his daughters be presented in the same Season. Understandable from the point of view of an elderly man who disliked leaving his home and journeying to a London that was incompatible with his temperament, but disastrous for the hopes of his eldest daughter. Emily would shrivel in the ridicule of London Society's malicious humor, while Daphne, with the advantages of her vivacity, wealth and pluck, would sail through without a scratch. No, a shy flower such as Emily would be crushed underfoot. She was really quite like a violet, quiet and sweet but so elusive that one must search hard to distinguish her charms. Just right for George, but not right for what was ahead of her.

"So I thought that if she was already engaged, she could come and have all the fun of a Season without any of the worry. We wouldn't be competing in any way, and I could . . ." She stopped with a guilty start.

He grinned at her, his thoughts like lightning. "And you could have yourself a rollicking good time, with your dowry and looks to attract suitors, and your vitality to enjoy all the attention you will undoubtedly receive."

"Well, yes."

"It's quite a good idea. I'm surprised that someone else hasn't thought of it."

"I think it may have occurred to Mama, but she is so very proper. She would hate for it to be thought that she had pursued George in any way."

"Pushy mamas are terribly disagreeable," he agreed.

"And so I have taken it upon myself to do what I can."

"Excellent. By the way, how old did you say you are?"

"Sixteen."

"Surprising."

"I had thought," again, she was blushing furiously, "but, I too, don't wish to seem to be encroaching, but I just thought . . ."

"You just thought?"

"That you might consent to help me. You see, I can

say things to Emily quite easily, in fact, I've been doing so for weeks and weeks, but your cousin George . . ."

"Is quite a different prospect. It would be most improper for you to say anything to George," he agreed hastily.

"Most improper."

"And I'm sure that you have your sister, in fact, the whole of your family, wrapped around your little finger, doing things they aren't even aware of."

"Yes, I suppose I do."

"But it isn't as easy with George."

"Not at all."

There was a pause, and he was amused to see that she was holding her breath, waiting for his answer.

"I would be glad to tender you my humble service," he announced, a pleased smile on his face.

She let her breath out. "Good!"

5.

The following afternoon, Max and Daphne were able to put their heads together and scheme.

Lady St. Wilfred had thought to send her daughters with a basket of fruit to an elderly maiden lady, the niece of a long deceased rector of the parish, and by some mystery, George and Max had been happening along the same path and asked to join the girls. The groom accompanying the sisters had fallen back to a discrete distance, no mean feat considering the slow pace Emily set for her mount, and Daphne, ever speedy, drew out ahead with Max by her side. Emily and George would cope with the basket as best they could.

It was a glorious day for a gallop. The grassy verge through the forest was too tempting a short cut to ignore, and the sun-filled sky over their heads was like a flag waving them on ever faster. Only when their horses were beginning to show signs of being winded did they slow down and bother with their mission.

Daring rescues? A duel! Some near fatal illness for George to succumb to, so that Emily could nurse him back to health. Daphne was full of ideas for throwing the couple together, Max more prosaic. They argued happily, enjoying a glorious time in their tenuous privacy, ignoring the need to reach an agreement, and in fact finding none.

The night before, Max had considered his rash promise to Daphne, and comforted himself with what justifications he could for interfering in his cousin's life. He, too, felt that Emily and George were well matched, and already fond of one another in their quiet, undemonstrative way. It would improve Emily's peace of mind in the coming Season if this match were settled before her departure for London. And finally, he felt justified in seeking some method of restraining Daphne. Left to her own devices, the girl would wreak havoc in the Anglian countryside.

If he had been applying this same fine logic to the situation as he rode and argued with Daphne, he would have wondered at the ease with which they found themselves alone. No sister, no groom, in fact, no chaperone at all dogged their heels. . . .

"Surely they have been alone together for quite a sufficient length of time, George. In fact," Emily added with a blush, "I fear that I have been sadly negligent in my duty to my younger sister, to leave her alone in a gentleman's company for so long. What Mama would think if she were to know, I cannot guess!"

"Dear Emmie, please don't distress yourself. My cousin is at all times the most careful and considerate of gentlemen when a young lady's honor is at stake. He will do nothing to discompose or agitate your little sister, of that I can assure you."

"Yes, yes, I have no doubt of that. It is not what I fear." In answer to his look of surprised enquiry, she continued, "What if your suspicions are not in fact the case? Your cousin is the first gentleman of fashion Daphne has spent much time with. It would not be beyond the bounds of imagination for her to fancy she has lost her heart to him, given her inexperience. Not that I would want you to think I suspect your cousin of any unseemly actions that might encourage such an attachment, far from it. But what if she falls in love with him, and not he with her?"

"My dear friend, your fears are natural and do your heart justice, but we must seize this opportunity and make the most of it. I have never seen Max behave toward any young lady in the manner he has used toward your sister. Surely you noted the glances he cast her way at table last night? And later, why, they were deep in conversation for quite half an hour, sitting on the window seat together.

"I have detected no hint of flirtation or any of the less agreeable attitudes that gentlemen of fashion all too often strike when dealing with damsels. From this alone, I am sure that Max has discovered something quite new to him. Daphne is so fresh! So free of coquetry! It is a rare experience for him, I assure you." He frowned down at his reins then continued in a disapproving voice. "I regret that it is necessary to expose my cousin, the head of my family, to you in this way, but I do so only to assure you that his conduct has been extraordinary. He is usually far less engrossed, far less attentive, and, well, far more, I fear I must admit it, far more flirtatious."

She looked at him without surprise, for she had guessed as much from her own observations and the casual scraps of gossip that had fallen her way during the visits of her mama's fine London friends. "But she is so young. Far too young for this match you contemplate to be a wise one."

"Nonsense. Max, for all his worldly airs, is but eight and twenty. His sophistication comes not from age but from the harsh experience of vast wealth and high title. To do him justice, the snubs and put-downs he administers are too often deserved by his victims. He has been pursued by marriage-minded young ladies and their mamas in a manner that I can only call vulgar."

Emily again nodded her understanding. "Daphne is not yet seventeen," she reminded him gently.

"And she is bright and lively and far older than her years. Your parents have allowed her a degree of freedom that has banished any missish ways. She is of an age to be molded by her husband, never a bad thing." He sounded pleased with this last.

She ignored his sententious tone. "But I do so want her to be happy!"

George reached over to squeeze her hand. "You are truly a most generous and noble woman. For all your ignorance, ignorance quite proper for one of your station and age, you have an understanding and sensitivity that make you see deeply into the hearts of others. It is for this, more than anything else, that I . . ."

Emily, her eyes demurely cast down, waited expectantly. Her companion flushed deeply, then turned his face away from her waiting figure. "Forgive me, I have said too much." Once again, she felt a queer pang of disappointment jab through her.

"George—Mr. Wade-Hambledon—you need offer me no apology. If I have but a fraction of the insight with which you credit me, I would know your motives to be generous."

He took courage from the warmth of her tone and turned back to her. "Then I ask for your help. I cannot explain this all to you now, but if my cousin and your sister do seem to form an attachment for one another, or if it seems wise to encourage such a thing, if they were to marry, well, in such a case, I could, I mean, we could . . ." His hesitation lengthened.

"You would very much like to see your cousin married and happily settled. Is that what you wish to say?"

"Yes. Not only for his sake, but . . ." Again, he was unable to finish his thoughts.

"But also for your own. You needn't fear the appearance of self-interest in my eyes. I know you have no ambition to step into his shoes and assume the burden of his wealth and title, a sentiment of which

51

you can be proud. But that would be your lot if he were to remain unmarried, without a son of his own to follow after him."

"You do understand! If he were married, I would feel free, free to choose my own life."

Emily ignored her sinking heart. "Of course. If I were somehow in your position, an impossibility, of course, but I use it to explain myself, I would feel just as you do."

"Then you will help me do what I can for them?"

"Need you ask? But now you must understand my scruples in the matter. I think that it's past time we rejoin them. I must attempt to preserve the proprieties, even as I assist you with your task." Her sweet smile told him that she meant no criticism with this insistence, and he seized her hand again and squeezed it.

"I am fortunate to be able to turn to you now. You are the ideal judge of taste and decorum. Whatever you feel would be right for your sister, I shall accept without a murmur."

Thus happily agreed, they allowed their mounts to lengthen their strides. Soon, the two couples, with the groom still in the background, sedately reached their destination.

6.

"And I must match those pink flowers with ribbons of the same shade, don't you recall, Emily? I have meant to refurbish that straw bonnet ages past to make it a bit more gay," Daphne explained cheerfully as she skirted the limb of a bramble bush that had overflowed into her path.

"But I fail to see that such a venture requires so many of us to attend on you, Daphne!" her gentle sister protested.

"We have to help her carry it all back," Max murmured.

"Carry it all back? Surely you jest, cousin!" George exclaimed. " 'Tis but a few trifles ..."

"Yes, it is an awesome load," Max said before the other man could finish his thought. "You can't expect

Miss Daphne to manage all those ribands and silk threads and lengths of muslin by herself, can you? Not to mention the packages from the apothecary shop, and the book she fetches from the vicarage for Sir Wilfred?"

The younger man looked unconvinced and inclined to argue as he shot a glance at the strong, upright figure of the healthy young woman in question, when he lurched in the path. A yelp escaped his lips.

"Careful, George," Daphne called out. "Those brambles have sharp thorns."

"Now she tells me!"

"Serves you right for questioning me, cousin," Max said sardonically. "You sounded almost human for a moment."

"George, I mean, Mr. Wade-Hambledon, have you injured yourself?" the older girl asked as she leaned over the entangled leg.

"It is but a scratch, Miss St. Wilfred. Please do not concern yourself with it. It is far more important that you avoid the thorns. Please, have a care!"

"But it could become infected, sir. It must be exceedingly painful!"

"It's well you wore your boots today, George. You shouldn't suffer unduly," his senior commented, addressing the sky. "I doubt much could get through that thick leather." Emily paid him no heed and knelt before the injured man, plucking at the entangling thorns with quick, gentle fingers. The others waited patiently.

They had traveled some two miles through fields

and an occasional plantation of trees as they made their way to the hamlet nearest St. Wilfred's Close. Flowers filled the fields, birds flitted through the trees and white clouds scudded across the blue skies, carried by some distant wind bearing inland a hint from the seas. It made the pause an agreeable one and Max found himself enjoying the view with his back turned on his cousin and the ladies.

"Come on!" this from Daphne, who had found her way to the top of the small hill that was the last barrier between them and their goal, the village of Wilfred Abbey. "We are almost there!"

As they crested the hill there was little enough to see of the village: only one twisted, rutted lane bordered closely by huddled cottages at one end and widening at the other into a ragged commons that offered an illusion of spaciousness to the vicarage and the small Georgian church placed across from it. The church was the most recent construction in the village, erected nearly fifty years before by a previous St. Wilfred whose conscience smote him with the memory of his ancestor's perfidy in depriving the local inhabitants of a convenient place of worship centuries ago when the Abbey was dissolved. When the new church was consecrated and its minister installed in a rambling stone house nearby, there was no longer any need for the Close's chapel to be opened to all and sundry. The common folk could mark Sundays and feast days in the village among their own kind, a far more convenient arrangement for all concerned.

The village also boasted an apothecary who doubled

as surgeon and physician, finding most of his patients among the four-legged stock of the area, a shopkeeper who filled the shelves of his front room with such merchandise as he saw a need for, including bolts of linen and lace rumored inherited from his grandfather, and the humble cottage of a spinster who eked out a meager living by taking in sewing. For the rest, the cottages housed a handful of laborers who walked to their work in the neighboring fields and the fishermen who manned the small fleet of boats in the nearby cove. The only building that looked prosperous was the Cherry Tree Inn; even the church was shabby and neglected in comparison.

Beyond the village, situated on another rise of ground that served to shelter the small community from the winds coming in off the sea, rose a bleached stone tower and two crumbling walls, the only remains of what once was the original church for the community, dating back long before there was even a thought of an Abbey St. Wilfred.

"Well," Max murmured under his breath. "It was quite worth the trip, I'm sure, brambles and all."

"I know it isn't very grand, but that's not the point, is it?" Daphne hissed back, for her sharp ears had picked his words from the faint breeze stirring about them.

He grinned down at her. "No, not at all. And the purpose of the walk, the point, as you so aptly called it, seems to be taking care of itself quite nicely." He nodded toward the figures of Emily and George, the latter tenderly offering his hand to assist that young lady over a particularly deep rut. It had not rained heavily in the district for some days, so the land they had walked over was easily negotiated, but the dust rose in the dry air, making it debatable whether a few puddles and splashes of mud might not have been preferable.

Daphne's errands were completed with alarming speed, the pink quickly matched (a minor miracle, considering the selection available), the vicar able to find the requested volume with ease, despite the piles of books and manuscripts tumbling from his library shelves and onto tables and chairs and even the floor in no discernible order, and the apothecary just back from delivering a calf and eager to serve them. The packages were duly distributed among the group after a mere three quarters of an hour. Ladened, the quartet stood on the green, each with one package in hand, and looked at one another, waiting for the first suggestion that they should return to the Close. Daphne stared about her in desperation, refusing to catch anyone's glance. The courting couple must have more opportunity than a mere three quarters of an hour to enjoy one another's company.

"Well . . .," began George after clearing his throat several times.

"The tower!" Daphne exclaimed.

"The tower? Oh, yes, the original tower," Emily echoed in some confusion, her eyes meeting a telling glance from George.

"Lord Edenbury particularly wanted to inspect it. Have you forgotten, my lord?"

"Yes, I had."

"Sir!"

"It must have been all this formality that drove it from my brain! Surely we can dispense with lords and misters," he grumbled.

"It is but a brick lighthouse," Emily deprecated.

"Lighthouse? Not at all, Miss St. Wilfred!" George protested. "It is a fine example of Saxon ecclesiastical architecture. And made of clunch, not brick."

Max looked at him with alarm. "Clunch?"

"Clunch."

They were walking toward the point of controversy, compelled by some mysterious impulse that required a complete exploration and explanation of the tower for the visitor's amusement. Daphne set the pace.

"Er, what is clunch, George?" Max asked manfully, after scowling at Daphne's retreating back.

"Clunch is a mixture of stones, too small in themselves for building, and a mess of clay and mud and sticks. Sometimes shells are added in areas such as this, where there is access to the sea. The mixture was used in districts where quarrying was unheard of. Much of the rectory is of clunch, too."

"Ah. Most interesting."

"But I am sure that I once heard that the tower served as a lighthouse of sorts, to warn ships of the sand bar out there," Emily protested, defending herself.

"But one has only to look at the interior of the tower, and the remains of the walls of the edifice it served, only partial remains it is true, but there nonetheless, to see that this was once a church," George enthused, even more pompous than usual.

"It's said to be haunted!" Daphne offered with a delighted shiver.

"Nonsense. This is hallowed ground, or was."

"Perhaps there are some graves about!"

"It is true that I have never explored it myself," Emily apologized hoping to turn the conversation to more becoming channels. "It is unwise of me to accept rumor instead of fact."

"Mama didn't approve of our exploring it on our own," Daphne explained. "And no one would come with us except Willie, and he doesn't count."

"Then allow me to show you where I feel sure the altar once stood. And there is even some indication of a memorial chapel to a past patron or neighboring lord in the remains of the west wall. I have made a study of this sort of building and I think you will find this example of particular interest." George offered Emily his arm, leading her past Daphne, who stood by with her mouth hanging open at his unexpected erudition.

"Clunch!" Max hissed in her ear.

She stifled a laugh, unable to answer him.

"I hope that the view, at least, will prove worth the climb."

"It is, it is, I assure you. You can see way out over the channel. And over toward Wade Hall and Forbisher Grange. Magnificent!" she said to him.

When they reached the foot of the tower, he conceded to himself that she had been justified in her assessment of the setting. The breeze that had been gentled by the intervening hills as they stood in the village green was fresh and invigorating as it came in off the water. Below them was a thin strip of shingle beach with waves crashing in sending up their spray; behind them spread the rich green of tidy fields, hedgerows and copses that were arranged over the rolling land. Only in England could one gain the impression of a carefully wrought miniature when one looked over cultivated countryside, he thought with satisfaction. Every plot of land was manicured and neat, fitting tightly into the seams of small trees and bushes or the darker green of woodland. Generations of care had given the scene an air of make-believe. Surely no land could be this neat, this precise!

"I consider it probable that the church was founded in the first half of the tenth century," George was explaining happily to Emily, his voice booming down on them from a slit window in the tower. The other couple had already found their way up the remains of the stairs within. "It is remarkable how these steps are still safe to climb, even after all these years! More often, wood was used for the interiors."

"Oh?" Emily sounded lost.

"It would have rotted after all these centuries," he explained quickly. "Still, the stone has had ample time to crumble. Remarkable!"

"Oh."

Max turned his back to the tower with pointed deliberation and stared out to sea.

"Now, whatever can he mean about the steps being

usable?" Daphne mused as she approached the gaping doorway of the tower. "They didn't used to be, except for the bottom few."

"I thought you weren't supposed to visit this place!" Max accused with a laugh.

"Yes, well . . ."

The interior of the tower was delightfully cool after the hot rays of the sun, and Daphne began to climb with enthusiasm. "I've never been able to get up so high before," she explained before she passed George and Emily on the rough landing by the lowest window.

Her enthusiasm was more than George had bargained for.

"But Miss Daphne, do you think you ought to go so . . ." he began.

"Daphy, I'm not sure that Mama would want you to go up so high. It is all very well if one of the gentleman were to lead the way, but for you to go ahead, alone, like this . . ." Emily's voice trailed off. It was obvious that her warning, and George's, was going unheeded, or perhaps unheard.

"Allow me, Miss St. Wilfred," Max said with a grin as he bounded up the stairs after Daphne. "I shall see to her safety." Relieved, the older girl turned back to George.

"But I'm sure that there was once some rumor that this place was put to use as a lighthouse. It would serve admirably in such a capacity, standing as it does so near the sea, and on such high ground. Do you see my point?"

"Of course, Miss St. Wilfred. But I do assure you most earnestly that whatever purpose it has since been put to, this tower began as a church."

"Smugglers!" Daphne called down, her single word echoing eerily in the enclosed walls, putting a period to George's ponderous explanations.

"Smugglers? Do you mean to suggest that this building was put to some nefarious use?" he asked with dismay.

Daphne's face peered over the edge of a wide ledge in the wall. "Why not? They could see for miles around from up here. That's important, you know, to sight the arrival of the ship bringing them their cargo, and to be sure that the excise men weren't on the way to arrest them. It would be most handy, to my way of thinking."

"It is preposterous! To even hint that hallowed ground would be put to such a use is beyond the realm of imagination!" he sputtered up to her, his indignation ringing around the walls.

"It wouldn't be the first time such a thing has come to pass, George," Max said.

"But to make the house of the Lord, even a derelict one, into a hideout for criminal activities is the outside of . . ."

"Now, now, George. Not everyone has your finely-honed sensibilities in such matters," Max laughed.

Before the younger man could protest further, another call was heard from Daphne.

"Look! On the post road. A cloud of dust!"

"On the post road?" Emily asked, turning quickly toward the window nearest her that opened in the right direction.

"Perhaps it is only a rider," George suggested, crowding close to Emily at her window.

"Perhaps it is only a cloud of dust," Max suggested with a grin.

"It's too big to be only a rider, George," Daphne called, forgetting her formalities. "I think it is at least a coach and four."

"Who could it be?" Emily speculated.

"Few folk travel this way," considered George. "Sir Walter and Lady Burnett, perhaps?" he finally offered.

"Why is everyone so excited?" asked Max.

"It is a coach from London, cousin!"

"There! It has turned."

"So it has," Emily confirmed.

They sounded strangely disappointed after their initial show of enthusiasm.

"It is only the Forbishers," Daphne explained to a puzzled Max.

George shook his head. "A pity. Now, Sir Walter is a fine, rational man, well read, with a firm knowledge of the world. A fine conversationalist, with a magnificent wine cellar. You would have enjoyed meeting him, Max." He sounded almost wistful.

"And Amy Burnett is in her first Season," sighed Daphne. "It would have been fun to hear her tales of London."

"It was silly of us to guess that it might be they for

that very reason," murmured Emily. "It is May, and the Season hardly half through. And they will be going to Brighton this year, I am sure."

"I enjoyed Sir Walter's visit at Christmas immensely," George added with a sigh.

"Whatever is this all about?" Max wanted to know. "I have stood quite enough of your babble! Now I want an explanation."

"New faces," Daphne said succinctly.

"Someone who has been in the outside world, the world beyond our little community," George explained more fully.

"Which is not to say that you have not enlivened us with your presence, m'lord," Emily hastened to add, in fear that they had insulted him. "It is only that countryfolk enjoy the company of newcomers to their ranks." She, too, was sounding wistful.

"Then what is wrong with the Forbishers?"

"Oh, well. They're just the Forbishers. Lady Forbisher, perhaps. Her husband rarely comes down with her."

"No one worth talking to," George mourned.

"They stay to themselves."

"Stuck up," finished Daphne, summarizing the situation for them all, once again with the fewest words possible.

And so the three of them, Daphne and Emily and George, turned their backs to the landward view, sighed deeply, and wore their disappointment as best they could, little knowing how wrong they were.

7.

"We shall begin with something simple, dearest Gerard," Lady Forbisher explained once again to her nephew. She had been whiling away the long hours of their journey by planning a series of lavish entertainments, outlining them in some detail to her traveling companion.

"Something simple," he yawned.

"A tea. Just the thing for the ladies. And, of course, you will meet them all. As my house guest, it would be only proper that you join us."

"Most proper." His pale gray eyes peered out from beneath swollen lids as he turned his attention to the window and the slowly passing scene it revealed.

She scowled at him. "I have heard that Miss Daphne is a most charming girl."

"And rich, very rich," he added with the only show of interest, a faint one, he had expressed the entire journey.

"Of course. Though we must go about this in a sensible manner," Lady Forbisher scolded.

"Dearest aunt, you know you can rely on me! As I rely on you."

"You had better! After all, you're the one who needs the money, darling."

"Don't we all?" he answered with a teasing smile.

Seeing that she was still pouting, he reached out to clasp her kid-covered hand. "Do tell me about this heiress once again, just so that I am sure I understand it all. It would be a pity if your brilliant discovery were to be wasted for lack of a little careful preparation on my part."

"Exactly!" she gasped, still a tiny bit angry that he was so blatantly pandering to her. After all, she had been repeating herself the whole of the journey for just that purpose. Then he smiled at her, a practised smile that hid the small gap between his two front teeth, and her indignation melted away.

Gerard Gascoigne eased his shoulders deeper into the plush upholstery of his aunt's well-padded, well-sprung traveling coach, and made every appearance of listening to her recital, but his mind was far away, in the London of unsavory Pall Mall gaming clubs and backstreet dives.

Gascoigne had inherited a comfortable competency on the death of a great-uncle some five years ago. Then a young man of twenty, with a family background that was well bred but by no means distinguished, and an education suitable for a gentleman, he had seized upon this capital and proceeded to live a life of extravagant frivolity that soon verged into the foolhardy and licentious. After a few months, only the highest flying ladies of the demimonde were sufficiently amusing to foil his ennui, the most outrageous wagers could tickle his fancy, the most extreme and expensive modes of fashion suit his image of himself. Within two years, the bulk of his estate had been dissipated, but the habits established in this wasting were firmly entrenched in his psyche. What had at one time been a style of living to be envied from a distance had come to be seen as a birthright. After his money was gone, he continued on the path he had chosen for himself, aided at first by extraordinary good luck. Dame Fortune had smiled on him at the tables, on the turf, even in the mean, dirty taverns where he attended cockfights and ratting contests. His winnings allowed him to pass for a man of wealth and property. Never for a moment did he allow himself to consider just how precarious his position was.

Not even when he began to lose rather more frequently than he had before, when there was less ready cash to be swept into his pocket after a night of faro or whist, did he mind his situation. Instead, he plunged more heavily than before, and memories of his early spectacular success encouraged others to extend to him whatever credit he sought. Soon he was losing more than he won, finally winning was a rarity, and notice was taken in certain quarters that good old Gascoigne's luck had turned. Credit disappeared, discreetly, quietly, very politely. But it was gone, leaving him with a pile of debts. Only the ladies, remembering the periods of lavish generosity that had marked his better days, a generosity maintained at the expense of unwary tradesmen whenever possible, failed to drop Gascoigne. He was still impeccably dressed, still charming and amusing, still the ideal gentleman to include in that intimate dinner party when one more man was needed—unless you had a marriageable daughter on your hands. Gascoigne found himself drifting into the society of dashing young matrons tied to rich, often elderly men, who were willing to be generous in their turn in exchange for certain attentions. The more respectable elements of Society, including the few relatives left him, tended to steer a course well away from him.

His Aunt Forbisher was an exception. In many ways, she exemplified to perfection the sort of lady who still kept him on, a dashing, married lady not overly concerned with her marriage vows and still young enough to be avid in her pursuit of pleasures. Although she was a mere ten years older than her nephew, their relationship was solely one of mutual assistance, for she often provided him with a gift of cash and he lied to her husband about her whereabouts during critical periods. Gerard had grown to be quite fond of her over the past year or so, and in fact had been relying on her hospitality after he had been turned out of his rooms in James Street. She was a gay little thing and still quite pretty, with pale eyes, so like his own, and a still girlish figure and skin. Only the cool gleam that one saw occasionally in those slightly protruding eyes seemed to have hardened with the passing years, but it was such that one could hardly notice it unless one knew her well, and it detracted not a whit from her charm.

The eyes had become positively flinty when he had finally told her he would have to leave London, perhaps for the Continent if that were possible, or the Colonies if worse came to worse. It was then that she had taken his affairs in hand. Bills were ignored, of course, for who cared about mere tradesmen, but some push was made to cover the gambling debts he had accrued, and it was she who had suggested the ultimate solution to his problems.

"So you see, this St. Wilfred girl is the very thing," she said, as the coach lurched to a halt at the foot of a broad sweep of shallow steps that climbed to the Doric columns of the portico girding the entire front of Forbisher Grange.

"Of course," Gerard murmured as he leapt to the ground and extended his hand to assist her to alight before the footman had even reached his post. She smiled fleetingly at him, and gave his fingers a warning squeeze as she swept up the steps to the open door. But in a moment they were alone again in the library, awaiting a soothing glass of wine to refresh them after their long journey, their luggage on its way upstairs.

"She has inherited the Roehampton mansion in London, and I heard that the whole of Mrs. Roehampton's fortune, which is as you well know considerable, will go to her on her marriage."

"Yes, but will it be enough?"

She arched her eyebrow at his sardonic tone. "Even for you, it should do," she snapped. "How you could have been so foolish as to let things come to these straits, I cannot imagine. You should have started looking for a wife long ago. It would have solved everything."

"Except that I would have undoubtedly long since run through her fortune."

"Gerard!"

"Yes, darling," he answered, meekly enough.

"You will try, won't you? None of this flippancy?"

"You have my word of honor. You are quite right, as always. This is the only way to go about it. You are absolutely a genius to have thought of it all." He leaned over and kissed her lightly on the cheek.

"It would be a wonderful coup, if you were to carry her off, love," she whispered, her eyes glinting hugely at him. "She hasn't even seen her first Season, and is quite unknown. No one else will have had a chance at her!"

"I shall snap her up, on sight, never fear. Even if I must close my eyes while I'm doing it to avoid what I might see."

"You need have no fear of that, silly! She should be a pretty little thing. Both of her parents are handsome and I did see her once myself, very briefly."

"And?"

"It was some time ago, and just in passing, you

know, but for a little girl she was most pleasing."

"No squint?"

"None. A really pretty smile and charming manners. Just the thing for you!"

"A limp? A hunched back?"

"Gerard!"

He sighed. "Perhaps I can leave her in the country for most of the year. It would be a pity to have a country bumpkin tied to me with apronstrings while in Town."

"Trust me!"

"But . . ."

"You will do as you please, once you are married to her, Gerard. But first things first."

"A tea!"

"Yes."

"How insipid."

"This is the country, after all! We shall begin there. Then a friendly visit, perhaps you could go riding with her, that sort of thing. You look remarkably handsome on a horse. And we might have a ball, just a country affair, but a ball nonetheless."

"Won't they be curious about all this sudden affability on your part? I had rather thought you ignored your neighbors down here. Your sociability might raise some eyebrows."

"Don't worry about that. They will be eager for a glimpse of the *ton*. And I can be useful to them. They have another girl to get off their hands."

"A little sister?"

"An older one. For some inexplicable reason, they

have delayed her first Season. She will be all the harder to get rid of for that. They'll be grateful for my help, once they get to London."

"Would you really do something for them there?"

"Perhaps. After all, she would be in the family then."

They smiled at one another across the room and he reached for one of the glasses the butler had just carried into the salon, handing the other to Lady Forbisher. As the servant closed the door behind him another thought sprang into Gascoigne's mind, one to make him pause. Noticing his arrested movement and sudden frown, Lady Forbisher turned to him with raised eyebrows.

"Well?"

"Well. While we have been gaily plotting my marriage with the delectable Miss St. Wilfred, we have failed to consider one important factor."

"And what is that?" she asked indulgently, sure of herself and her generalship.

"What if she already has a beau? Or even a fiancé?"

"A beau? She hasn't even been to Town yet."

"But she could well be acquainted with some local farmer and be prepared to marry near home."

"Whatever do you mean?"

"Competition, my dear aunt. Competition," he said harshly. "You have assumed that I shall be the only knight to enter the lists for the fair lady's favors. Can you be so certain? A fortune such as you describe would attract a fair amount of attention, I should think. Just look how it has brought me all the way from London. Surely there are eligible, and ineligible, bachelors nearer at hand who have begun to woo her."

Her eyes glared terribly for a moment, then she visibly calmed herself and considered this possibility. "There is George Wade-Hambledon. He is a bachelor and eligible enough." There was a pregnant pause while she weighed the situation. "But he is so very proper! Such a bore! And he's Edenbury's heir. He needn't hang out for a rich wife."

"The future Lord Edenbury? Heir to a marquisate? Then in all likelihood the family will be chasing after him."

"Perhaps. But you needn't worry, love." She was smiling again and patting his hand indulgently, seemingly vastly entertained with some private joke.

"Well? What's so funny?"

She chuckled again. "The vision of Wade-Hambledon paying court!"

"I don't see what you can mean by that! This is no laughing matter! I think you have dragged me all this way for nothing, dearest aunt." He turned his back on her, a sulky look deepening into a scowl.

By now she had started to laugh outright, pealing trills of amusement that were one of her chief charms. "But darling, marquisate or no marquisate, he is still no competition! The man is a dreadful bore! Pompous and dull! Why, I hear he even writes learned papers on Church history. And he never, never comes to London! What young girl would be interested in a stick in the mud such as he, when there is a dashing London blade nearby to turn her head?"

Gascoigne considered this for a moment and then turned to grin at her. "Of course. You are absolutely right. If you are sure that he is all I shall have to contend with, the thing is as good as done."

8.

"What a lovely garden, Lady Forbisher," Daphne said to her hostess as she balanced a cup of tea and plate of crumpets and sandwiches on her lap, her skirt and ankles prim, hands folded whenever not hovering over her food. Her hostess had insisted that the girl take the seat next to her on a small antique bench, and Daphne was doing her best to live up to this honor.

"Yes, I am quite proud of it. You must spend some time exploring it today before you leave." She smiled with what was a sincere pleasure in her youngest guest, for everything was going far better than her wildest hopes.

Her invitation to tea had been accepted with apparent alacrity by the St. Wilfred ladies, and Lady Forbisher had decided to expand her party to include the gentlemen. After all, once dearest Gerard had met Wade-Hambledon, he would know that he had nothing to fear from that quarter. The information that this gentleman had a houseguest, and that the guest was his distinguished relative the Marquess of Edenbury, guaranteed that she, too, would enjoy herself. She had long wanted to improve her acquaintanceship with his lordship, and pressed for his inclusion in her party.

When the day had dawned so beautifully bright and clear, she had determined to serve her tea al fresco, hoping for just such an opportunity to arise as Daphne's suggestion had now presented. With everyone scattered along the hedged paths, almost anything was possible. She smiled at Edenbury.

"Perhaps my nephew could escort Miss Daphne through the walk," she suggested with a hint of a guileful smile. "And I would be honored to show his lordship my greenhouse."

"I'm sure that Lady St. Wilfred and I would enjoy such a tour," his lordship answered with a smile and a bow in the older lady's direction. He was rewarded with a knowing look from that quarter.

"You are too kind, Lady Forbisher, to cater to my interest in horticulture," Lady St. Wilfred said with a cool little laugh. "I'm quite notorious among my friends for the boring lengths I go to when set down in the midst of a truly fine mass of flowers and plants. I fear they try to avoid the subject in my presence."

Lady Forbisher, already disappointed by Edenbury's inclusion of another guest in her proposed tour, smiled even more doubtfully. "I fear that there is really very little to interest an enthusiast such as yourself, Lady St. Wilfred."

"On the contrary," her guest countered. "Your greenhouse enjoys an enviable reputation in these parts."

"Then we shall explore the walks while you tour the greenhouse," Daphne said with decision.

Lady St. Wilfred hesitated slightly, then glanced at Emily. "That sounds a fine plan. It would be a pity to coop up such youthful spirits on a day as lovely as this. I'm sure that Emily and Mr. Wade-Hambledon will quite enjoy your little expedition."

Daphne was already on her feet. "Then we must begin! I've heard of your wonderful maze, Lady Forbisher, and intend to learn its riddle!" she said gaily, throwing a secret grin at Max.

"And I shall be your guide, Miss Daphne," Gascoigne murmured through his close-lipped smile, his eyes lingering over the figure of the vibrant girl beside him.

"What? Oh yes, of course, Mr. Gascoigne. Very kind. Unless you should prefer the greenhouse . . . No? Oh, well, Emily, George, come, we must start on the maze." And with this she swept her party off with the air of a commanding general leading his troops on a sortie.

The older members of the party watched their departure with varying degrees of discomfort. Max was admiring Daphne's energy in seizing an opportunity for George and Emily to be paired off, but he could only hope that she would not let her enthusiasm carry her away. After all, George had a nice sense of what was pleasing. Lady Forbisher was wishing she could suggest that Lady St. Wilfred accompany her eldest daughter as a chaperone, while leaving the younger to Gascoigne's tender attentions. And Lady St. Wilfred, having spent most of the tea carefully observing Gerard Gascoigne without appearing to be anything less than totally charmed by him, wished that Lady Scorby was there to advise her. She strongly suspected that the Scorby list of fortune hunters was one short of being complete.

"I am not at all sure that I wish to enter the maze, Daphy," Emily said with surprising firmness. "It would be dreadful to get in and not be able to find your way out."

"Don't be such a ninnyhammer, Em! I'm dying to see it."

"Then I shall escort just Miss Daphne through the puzzle, Miss St. Wilfred," Gascoigne offered quickly, one arm already bent to accept the burden of Daphne's hand. "You and Mr. Wade-Hambledon may prefer to linger among the roses."

"I wonder that you do not join the party in the greenhouse, Daphne," George said. "I know how fond you are of flowers." Gascoigne's eyes narrowed as he heard the informality of this address, and he waited to see just what Wade-Hambledon was planning.

"Flowers?"

"Yes, Daphne, I think George's idea is a famous one. You ought to visit the greenhouses this afternoon, with Mama and Max!" her sister enthused, prompted by a nudge from George.

"And Lady Forbisher," he added hastily.

Gascoigne frowned. "Perhaps another day, when the weather hasn't graced us with such glorious blue sky and warm sun, I can take Miss Daphne through the greenhouse. But today is too fine to be wasted inside. It is perfect for the maze. And it will be oppressively hot under the glass, I am sure."

"Then the maze it is. Come on, Emily! George!"

Daphne turned toward the entrance to the neatly trimmed hedges as she spoke these words, Gascoigne at her heels, leaving her sister and George to sigh with exasperation.

"We must follow, I suppose," Emily said in a quiet aside to her companion.

"But of course! We can't allow her to wander about with that, that, with Mr. Gascoigne." George sounded shocked.

"We tried. You were very clever. I should never have thought to encourage her to visit the greenhouse! It would have been so natural for her to talk with your cousin there."

"We shall try again later."

They followed after the other couple, and soon the four young people found themselves confused in a series of twisting paths, culs-de-sac, and at one point, circular patterns that led them back onto their own footsteps. It was a beautiful day, and the sun was very pleasant, and soon they were laughing and joking, wondering if the gardeners would have to cut through the hedges to lead them out.

Emily had sunk to a small stone seat and was laughing and panting, with George hovering beside her, when Daphne struck out on a determined course of her own. Gascoigne was immediately on her heels.

"Daphy, don't go too far!" Emily called out.

"How can I? I shall probably be led back to you from the opposite direction," she laughed as she turned a corner. Then as the leafy hedges closed in around her and her companion, she suddenly picked up her skirts and ran, hissing, "Come on, don't dawdle so! We must lose them!"

Gascoigne, bemused by his unexpected success after a mere two hours of charming attention, followed her readily enough. In a moment Daphne had led them through so many turns in the maze they could have been miles away from the stone bench.

"There!"

"Yes, there!" He leaned nearer her, one hand reaching for her arm. "You look quite charming with the sun playing on your hair as it does, Miss Daphne. Or may I call you Daphne as Wade-Hambledon does?"

"George? I've known George forever. He's always called me Daphne, you know."

She moved away, ignoring, or perhaps not seeing, the wandering hand. But this failed to discourage him. He reached her side in two strides and slipped his hand up along her arm. "I am delighted to have this opportunity to be alone with you, Miss Daphne," he whispered into her hair. "What a clever girl you are to arrange it."

"It's not us I was thinking of, silly. Far from it," she said with a shrug as she moved again. "Now, let's look for a way out of here, one that won't take us past Emily and George, if we can manage it."

"Why bother to stray from this lovely glade! It is quite private and delightfully romantic. Of course, I quite concur with your desire to avoid the others.. What better place to accomplish it than here?"

"Do stop this flummery! I didn't come out here so that you could whisper idiotish things into my ear, Mr. Gascoigne," Daphne said with a hint of asperity.

"Then why did you come? You have been leading me a merry chase, miss," he said with a forced smile.

"I have been arranging for Emily and George . . ."

"To face the challenge of escaping this maze by themselves," a third voice said coolly from the end of the short alley they stood in. "You see, Mr. Gascoigne, my cousin and Miss St. Wilfred are both notorious for their lack of any sense of direction. Put them on the top of a hill facing the sea, and in five minutes they will have lost sight of it. Even with a compass and map, poor George couldn't find his way out of there. He's been known to get lost in the library of Wade Hall."

Standing there in his negligent riding attire, so inappropriate for a tea party but also very attractive, was Max Wade-Hambledon, a look on his face that was chilling Gascoigne to the bones despite the warmth of the air around them.

"What the . . . How did you get here?"

"Unlike my cousin, I have a superb sense of direction, Mr. Gascoigne. I can find anything I want to, even if it is hidden in the heart of a maze." Then he turned to Daphne, a hint of warning in his eyes. "Don't you think we should rescue the stranded couple? Surely they have been left to their own devices quite long enough."

"But . . ."

"We wouldn't want to cause them any real distress, Daphy. Now turn about, girl, and lead the way."

"Oh, very well."

And to Gascoigne's amazement, they were back at the bench in a few short minutes.

"Daphne, where have you been?" Emily began with a nervous start when she saw her sister approach. "We didn't know where to turn to look for you." She broke off as she saw the tall figure of Edenbury emerge from the hidden path.

"I have found Max here. He decided to try the maze too, after all, instead of the greenhouse."

"What! Oh, jolly good seeing you, old boy!" George exchanged a delighted glance with Emily and vigorously nodded his approval.

"Well, that sounds a bit extravagant, George, but it's nice all the same to feel wanted."

"Quite. Now, if we can just find our way out of here, Max! I am completely turned about, you know."

"George, you're sounding human again."

One set of conspirators held their council of war after the tea party broke up that afternoon.

"That damned Wade-Hambledon is certainly no competition, but I don't like the looks of Edenbury," Gascoigne growled to his aunt over a glass of Madeira.

"Wade-Hambledon is certainly smitten with the elder girl, which is just as well. But you needn't worry about Edenbury. He's far too old for the chit. He'd never throw his cap over the mill for a pretty little goosecap like her."

"Who said anything about a love match? You have explained the source of his interest already. It's the same as mine! She's an heiress!"

"And he's a rich man."

"Money never hurts, Aunt."

"Darling, you can rely on me to distract him from young Daphne," Lady Forbisher purred. "He only left the greenhouse to escape Lady St. Wilfred, you know."

"I'm not so sure of that!"

Her eyes snapped with anger, then she asked with a show of concern, "You're not giving up, are you?"

"Giving up?" An ugly gleam entered his pale blue eyes and they began to bulge every bit as much as his aunt's did. "No. I want that girl. And her money. And I intend to have both."

"Damn it, Daphne, you have to be more careful!"

"They were only alone for a few minutes, Max," she protested. "Do stop scolding."

"While they were alone, so were you."

"No, I wasn't. The nephew was with me."

"That's what I meant!" he said through gritted teeth.

She looked at him with surprise. "You mean *I* have to worry about being chaperoned, too?"

"Of course, you silly widgeon!"

"Oh! I'd never thought of that."

"You had better start considering it. Doubly so when that Gascoigne is about. Promise me, Daphne!"

"Well, I suppose I shall, since you ask it of me. But why?"

"He's just the sort to cause you unpleasantness!" Max explained stiffly. "I think we have the answer to your mother's curiosity regarding Lady Forbisher's sudden hospitality. She is seeking to introduce her nephew to you."

"You sound just like George!" she giggled. Then in honesty she had to add, "He was saying the silliest things, and whispering them into my ear, of all things! Whatever do you suppose he was up to?"

"Daphne, what do you think?" Max asked in despair. "Hasn't your mama taught you anything?"

"That? Oh!" She was giggling again. "How remarkably foolish lovemaking is. If that's all I have to resist, it won't be difficult at all."

9.

Mr. Gascoigne had been less than convinced by his aunt's assurances that Miss St. Wilfred was a charming girl of pleasing manners and appearance, as pretty as any London miss, in short, a young lady he would not find unattractive. He had strongly suspected his relative of practising guile, not that he would have blamed her for that. After all, she had his well being at heart. It would be like her to try to make a bitter pill more palatable with a little sugar coating.

But his impression of Daphne at the tea party far exceeded his most optimistic expectations. She was very pretty, and promised to grow into a striking beauty. Far from being henwitted, as he had fully believed all country misses to be from sheer proximity to the poultry runs, her conversation was bright and lively. No arch, simpering miss here. To his relief, he found himself charmed by her, making the seduction all the more pleasant for him. What was more important, her surprisingly free manners would make it easy.

And so it was more than necessity that speeded his determined courtship. The very next afternoon, he arrayed himself in his London finery, set his beaver hat at a rakish angle over one eye, and set out for St. Wilfred's Close. With his pale yellow pantaloons, sarsanet waistcoat covered with embroidered sprigs of blue periwinkles, and the biscuit-colored coat that had only just been delivered before he had departed London for his rustication, he presented almost too glamorous a figure for the East Anglia countryside to absorb. It was a pity that on arriving at the Close, the only pair of eyes there to appreciate his splendor belonged to old Silas, Sir Wilfred's head gardener. Silas seemed pathetically unimpressed.

"Sir Wilfred to be found on the stud farm," he answered gruffly when Gascoigne asked after Miss Daphne.

"It would please me exceedingly to have an opportunity to converse with Sir Wilfred, my good man, but on this occasion it is his daughter whom I seek."

"Lady St. Wilfred took Miss Emmie to vicarage. For tea. They no be back afore supper."

"Miss *Daphne,* my good man! It is Miss Daphne St. Wilfred of whom I speak. What sort of a chuckle-head are you?"

Silas looked up at him through bushy eyebrows, a

gleam in his rheumy eyes that Gascoigne failed to notice. "Miss Daphy?"

"Miss Daphne."

"Miss Daphy's about her business." He moved as if to turn away from these tiresome questions.

By now Gascoigne had dismounted of his own accord and handed the reins of his stallion to a stablelad who had ambled onto the scene. "Then you will have the butler inform her of my arrival," he ordered, turning toward the front door of the house.

The gleam was more pronounced. "Miss Daphy be out of doors."

"You will find her, you mutton-headed bumpkin, or you will soon know why you should have! Get to it!"

"She won't come in."

"Did you hear me?" All the polish of his manners had disappeared as he faced the kneeling servant, an ugly flush mounting his face.

The gardener, poking his spade at a lonely weed that had somehow become ensconced in the fine front lawn of the Close, ignored the order.

It was only an inspired thought of how he could turn this to his own advantage that prevented Gascoigne from lowering his riding crop on the old man's bowed shoulders. "Tell me where she is and I shall seek her out myself," he suggested with a return to better humor.

Silas squinted up at the crop hovering over his head, then pointed toward what was undoubtedly an appurtenance of the home farm, a rough field just visible from the house. "Miss Daphy went that away," and he poked again at the flourishing weed.

Gascoigne turned his back on this worthy without another word, once he had the information he wanted. A pleased smile on his face, he carefully picked his way along a path that seemed to take him in the direction he desired, his every care being for the shine of his Hessians amongst the rude shrubs and vines. After some fifteen minutes of mincing, he came to the field and vaulted over the fence, ignoring the stile. His arrival, despite its flourish, passed unnoticed.

"Miss Daphne, you look radiant!" he exclaimed as he came to within earshot of the girl. "I shall always remember you as I see you now, rising like a young dryad from the greenery!" He reached out as if to take her hand to kiss it, but was confounded to find her fingers clenched around some small object that disappeared into the pocket of her skirt.

Daphne, feeling neither radiant nor particularly dryad-like, merely hot, looked at him doubtfully. "This is a surprising honor, Mr. Gascoigne. I had not thought we would meet again so soon." Her tone was far from friendly, indeed, almost brusk.

Unabashed, he continued as he had begun. "I could not stay away! You cannot begin to imagine the impression you made on me yesterday at my Aunt Forbisher's party. You are as beautiful as any London belle, more so, in fact, but without the stiffness and hauteur one too often finds in such ladies. I had not imagined to find a diamond of the first water hidden away in the countryside. I congratulate you!"

"You must not throw the hatchet at me in such a way, sir!" she insisted, her tone cross.

If he was surprised at her ready command of cant terms, he hid it well. "I've no desire to indulge in idle flattery, Miss Daphne, for the very simple reason that I have no need to. I come only to tender to you my humble admiration and to offer any service you might require. If there is anything I might do for you, I beg of you that you be so kind as to tell me of it."

During this speech he had swept off his fine beaver hat, more for the purpose of showing off his thick curly hair than from any sense of manners. Daphne's eyes lit on the hat and at once her expression changed.

"You may be of help this instant, sir!"

"I am so humbly gratified," he smirked back. "How may I assist you? Do you need advice on your coming Season? I know what you must be feeling, the excitement, the trepidation! A few words from a gentleman who has always traveled in the first rank of the *ton* would be beyond price, I know. I am sure that you will find London a happy and exciting place. You may even want to settle there in a home of your own, once you have found a husband. If there is any advice, any at all, that I can offer, I shall be glad to do what I can. You must rely on me in all things, Miss Daphne!"

"London? I haven't been thinking of that at all!"

His poise, previously bolstered by the pleasant conviction that all was going even better than planned, was briefly ruffled. "What? Then what can it be? Ah, you require assistance in your search! You are looking for something out here, aren't you? If you will but tell me what it is you seek. ..." As he spoke, he took a step back, as if to better examine the ground around them, only to create an alarming sound. Something had shattered under his heel.

"Oh, no, how could you? You have broken another one. I see that I shall have to be careful where I let you wander!"

"Broken another?" He peered into the weeds around him, his eyes searching for a clue.

"Yes, and I was being so careful!"

He favored her with an uneasy smile.

"I don't quite . . ."

She ignored his words. "Hold out your hat. No, not that way, turn it over. Upside down!"

When he had obeyed her, she began searching the various pockets and folds of her costume, bringing out small objects she carefully deposited in his glossy hat.

"There! All safe. Now, don't drop them!"

Confused, Gascoigne peered into the folds of his headwear, hoping to discover what treasures lay there. His perplexity was only increased by what he saw there: a collection of brown eggs nesting warmly in the loose silk lining.

His voice sharpened. "Eggs?"

"Of course. The hens got out of their run yesterday afternoon, and were found this morning wandering in this field by one of the farmlads. He promptly stepped on three eggs as he shooed them back to their perches, so I offered to hunt for the rest of the eggs myself. And now you have stepped on a fourth!" She frowned her disapproval of his clumsiness and returned to a thick clump of weeds with something of a flounce.

For a moment Gascoigne forgot the purpose of his visit. Grasping his hat with both hands, he was in the act of tipping it right side up, regardless of the contents. Then the remembrance that his hatter's bill had not been paid in nearly a twelve-month held him, and he forced a smile.

"Eggs!" His tone was happier. "A treasure that must be destroyed before one can obtain its richness. So humble, yet hiding a wealth of gold past price."

Her eyes flew to his face and she stifled her first reaction to his eloquence. "What a charming way of describing them, Mr. Gascoigne. It is almost a riddle, I fancy."

"Something like that," he answered with a show of modesty.

"And so clever of you to think of it all by yourself! On the moment, so to speak."

" 'Tis nothing, nothing! A small thing when one considers my inspiration for it."

"I'm so pleased that you don't hold my egg hunt in disdain, sir. My brother Willie refused to help me! Can you imagine?"

"How unchivalrous of him."

"He even laughed."

"No! Surely not!"

She nodded her head vigorously to assure him that this was so, her solemn expression barely concealing a twinkle in her eyes. Then a wayward dimple cut the corner of her mouth and Gascoigne was positively preening himself. Stifling laughter once again, she turned to a small bush that was growing in the middle of the field. Gascoigne, seeing this as a priceless opportunity to impress himself upon the girl without a chaperone present, forged on.

"I see you are like Ceres, Miss Daphne. You preside over the riches of the fields."

"Ceres?" She frowned as she reached through some brambles for another egg. "Didn't she have something to do with grain? Or was it cereal? The words mean the same, I fancy. I'm not sure that grain and eggs are the same thing, though. Here." Another egg was thrust into his hat.

"They are both golden . . ." he began desperately.

The girl pressed her point despite this interruption. "And she was old, wasn't she? A mother, as I recall. Or did you mean the asteroid?"

"Asteroid?"

"Watch your step!"

He nearly fell over as he tried to retrieve his wandering left foot. Daphne's hand flashed into the grass and another egg appeared in her palm, only to be tucked away with the others. Feeling a little desperate, he stumbled back, only to be entangled in a runner of brambles.

"Ouch!"

"There, there, I'll get you out. Although how you can feel anything through those boots is anybody's guess. Don't fidget so, and for heaven's sake, don't squall!"

Affronted, as any gentleman of sensibility would be, but whether by the reference to his boots or by her description of his justifiable complaints it was impossible to tell, Gascoigne snapped back, "That damned bush brushed my leg well above the knee!"

"Now, now, you mustn't be offended, sir. We deal in plain terms here in the country. I should have realized that something like this would happen. You are ill-equipped for a jaunt in a field. Anyone can see with half an eye that you're a 'man of the Town'!"

He was left at *point non plus,* unsure of the exact meaning to ascribe to her words. Surely she wasn't calling him a libertine? To his face? No, no. She was too young, too innocent to know the meaning of such things. Then he recalled her earlier use of cant terms and was thrown into doubt once again.

"You are every bit the London gentleman in your fine clothes. Those polished Hessians aren't at all the thing for these briars and brambles, are they?"

Reassured by the tone of admiration he fancied he detected in her voice, he glanced down with complacency at his apparel. He *did* look rather fine, he knew. She had meant to compliment him. But before he could say more, an appalling sight met his eye.

"They are scratched! Both of them!" He pointed down to his boots, his pose fraught with all the drama and intensity of an Old Testament prophet. "They are ruined! Ruined!"

She sat back on her heels and stared hard at the damage. "Oh, dear! What a pity. Perhaps your man will know of something that can be done. Why don't we give up hunting for eggs now, Mr. Gascoigne? I have found an even dozen, in any case. That should please Cook." She turned toward the stile, waving for him to follow, hat in hand. If she heard him muttering his breath, she gave no hint of it.

After considerable difficulty, she got him over the fence, for he was now morbidly conscious of the damage done to his boots, so much so that it seemed to affect the use of his lower limbs. Daphne finally rescued the hat and left him to scramble over as best he could. She was not surprised when he evinced no interest in dallying longer in her company, and in truth she failed to extend an invitation that he do so.

As the eggs were being transferred from the loosened lining of his hat to a basket provided by the cook, Sir Wilfred arrived on the scene. Poor Gascoigne, anxious to be off to lick his wounds in peace, stumbled through a parody of well-mannered farewells.

"Alas, that I cannot linger to converse with you, sir!"

"Pity!"

"A mere friendly visit . . ."

"Quite."

"As a neighbor, albeit a temporary one . . ."

"Most kind."

"To affirm my kindest regards for your daughter . . ."

"Oh?"

"And her family, of course!" he added in misery, sure that Sir Wilfred was staring at his boots and mentally characterizing him as a shabrag.

Sir Wilfred, who was staring at the whole of his

guest's apparel with a lively interest uninspired by the boots, vouchsafed a gruff, "Thankee," to this.

As he heard these words, Gascoigne raised his hat to his head, as if to set it firmly in place with a smart tap. But something arrested his movement and a sickly look crossed his face. Sir Wilfred watched with interest, wondering what further antics this Bond Street lounger would perform for their entertainment, but Gascoigne merely steadied his hat with a gulp and a weak smile and turned to his mount without so much as an adieu.

Once alone with his daughter, Sir Wilfred turned to her and spoke with some asperity. "What a loose fish he is. Did you see the look on his face at the last? And he rode off without so much as a good-bye, after all that pother."

"He is quite a perfect cabbagehead, Papa. You should have seen him in the field! He may be a fine gentleman in London, but here he's ridiculous!"

"You just be sure not to encourage that one, Daphy, for all his fine manners, or I'll take you over my knee. He's a bad 'un, a here-and-thereian, if ever I saw such a case!" Saying this, he took the basket from her and began poking at the eggs.

"He seemed a mere bobbing-block to me, Papa!"

"Well, just you remember that if ever you should meet him again in Town!"

"You need have no fear of that." She smiled at him, the mischief showing through again. "He was terribly kind, though. He helped me gather the eggs!"

"Pooh! You can't make me believe that he didn't step on all of them!"

She rushed to Gascoigne's defense. "Only one!" Then her incurable honesty forced her to add, "And nearly another, but I stopped him in time to rescue it."

"Goosecap! That just goes to prove what I've said. He was worthless, wasn't he? Silly of you to ask him for help."

"Worthless? He was no such thing! I put all the eggs in his hat. A dozen of them. It was just the thing!"

"What was that, you addledbrained puss?" he asked with a scowl for the basket. "How many did you find?"

"A dozen. Exactly!"

"But there are only eleven here now."

"Well, there were twelve in the hat when we left the field. I'm sure of it."

"Odd."

"Cook will just have to make do."

"Still . . ." He stared at her, then at the thin cloud of dust that was all that was left of Mr. Gerard Gascoigne's visit. A pleased grin spread over his face and in a moment his daughter, following his look and then his thoughts, joined in his laughter.

Gascoigne could have answered the riddle of the missing egg if he had chosen to. Instead, shielded behind a convenient hedgerow, he was diligently wiping the remainder of the treasure beyond price from his head and face, where it had deposited itself when it fell from its hiding-place in the lining of his hat.

10.

"I am not precisely sure that it is wise for me to be accompanying you on this expedition, Daphy," Emily said in a tremulous voice as she clung to her saddle, the other hand tangled in the reins.

"Nonsense. You'll enjoy yourself immensely, I'm sure. Don't you agree, Mr. Gascoigne?"

Gascoigne, who was wishing Emily to the devil, or at any rate someplace other than at her sister's side, murmured something incomprehensible. The memory of the egg fiasco had been pushed brusquely from his mind, and his aunt's suggestion the next day that he invite their young neighbor out for an afternoon's ride had seemed a sensible one. He was greeted with flattering enthusiasm when he arrived at the Close, only to find his invitation amended to include an unwilling Emily. As he had intended the ride to be an intimate tête-à-tête designed to give him an opportunity to impress the heiress with his fine seat on a horse and his other manly charms, he was less than pleased to find his *ménage* now *à trois*, and moving at a snail's pace.

"What did you say, Mr. Gascoigne? The wind has blown it away," Daphne asked.

"Lovely day for a ride."

"It is not that I can't enjoy the day, Daphne, it is very pretty. It is the riding that troubles me," Emily continued with a gulp and a lurch.

"Now, Emily, you can't expect us to swallow that clanker! You ride quite well enough, as you should know. Just lift your reins a bit and let go of the pommel. Your little mare is a sweet stepper, she will give you no trouble. You did fine last week with George!"

Emily trembled in response.

While this exchange was being made, Gascoigne had noticed that their route had somehow diverged from what he had planned. In fact, Miss Daphne was taking them in the wrong direction entirely, one that led farther inland.

"Miss Daphne, forgive me, but I had thought to follow a path to the beaches and then along them farther north of the village. Being a stranger to the district, I am most anxious to explore the shoreline. Of course, I rely on you to guide me there!" he explained with his suave charm while he tried to lead his mount back to his chosen path.

"We shall be there directly," the girl answered over her shoulder, refusing to be distracted to the other direction.

"But we are going the wrong way entirely!" he sputtered.

"Not to worry!"

"We are heading inland, toward Wade Hall," he said in a thunderstruck voice.

"Of course! I thought we might just see if Lord Edenbury and his cousin would like to join us."

"George? What a wonderful idea!" Emily said with the first enthusiasm she had displayed since Daphne had begun forcing her riding habit over her head earlier that day, muffling the older girl's protests.

Daphne smiled to herself, pleased and a trifle arch at her own subterfuge. Max had warned her to be subtle and she was doing her best. Their pace quickened perceptibly as Emily took heart.

Gascoigne looked furious with this news. More company, especially when it took the shape of a marquess and his heir, competition no matter what his aunt claimed, was the last thing he wanted. He was so angry that his hands twitched convulsively, pulling hard at his mount's tender mouth. Neighing, the stallion skidded to a halt on his hind legs, almost rearing.

"Careful, sir. This is rough ground for such a display," Daphne warned, reaching out to take the distraught animal's reins and calm him, and paying no heed to Gascoigne's firm handling of the situation once he had put his mind to it. The horse was quickly calmed between their combined efforts and the pace resumed, toward the Hall.

Before he could remonstrate further regarding their destination, they had entered the tidy drive that led them to Wade Hall. Their path demurely followed a straight line through a plantation of young oak, wandering neither to the right nor the left as it made its way to the house. Then a farmhand leading a limping horse up the lane raised his hat and hallooed them, and there was no turning back.

The master of Wade Hall was out on his front portico to greet them when they arrived. "My dearest Miss St. Wilfred, I must assist you to dismount. Please, allow me!" he said anxiously after perfunctory greetings to Emily's companions. He was as aware as the rest of the neighborhood that she was not a notable horse-woman. Daphne could be left to take care of herself.

Not that she need have worried, for Max appeared from the direction of the kennels and offered her a strong arm before Gascoigne had managed to untangle his horse's reins and get to her side. "Down you go, easy! Now, why have you dragged your poor sister out for a ride? It was most unkind of you," he scolded with easy familiarity.

"Not at all. When she arrives in London for her Season, she must be prepared to ride in the Park during the fashionable promenade, isn't that so, Mr. Gascoigne?"

Stifling an angry retort, that gentleman smiled and agreed. "Although perhaps Miss St. Wilfred would prefer to appear in a gig or carriage. That is also done by many of the ladies."

Daphne pouted her disdain. "How poor-spirited of them! And it won't do for today. We want you all to come with us for a canter down the beach. You can't do that in a gig. What do you say, George? Max?"

"A canter?" Emily gasped, clinging to George's arm while a groom took the reins from her limp fingers. Daphne's informality went unheeded.

"Well, maybe a trot," the girl amended.

"We shall be delighted to join you," Max said immediately, grinning at Daphne.

"We shall do no such thing!" George protested sharply, steadying Emily while a worried frown spread over his face. "A further ride is quite out of the question. Out of the question! Especially one so dangerous as to involve a canter!"

"Fine," Max answered, drawing a horrified look from his cousin. George had only then realized that he had contradicted, perhaps for the first time in the whole of his life, the man to whom he owed every consideration and courtesy.

"That is, I mean to say . . ."

Gascoigne interrupted him. "Please don't concern yourselves with my little outing. Miss St. Wilfred can rest here while Miss Daphne and I trot down to the beach. Yes, that is just the thing! Capital idea!"

Hearing this, George and Emily drew themselves up and stiffened their backs.

"It is very kind of you to consider my welfare, Mr.

Gascoigne, but there is no reason for me to stop here to rest. I am not the least tired," Emily said firmly. "I shall, I shall . . . I am quite looking forward to this ride, I assure you."

George, the quandary flung in his face, for it was against his principles for a young lady of rank to go gamboling about the countryside in the company of a man who was not her kinsman, in fact, a man of somewhat dubious character, if he was any judge, began to sputter.

"We shall all accompany you to the beach on your exploration, Mr. Gascoigne. But we shall ride at a decorous pace, one suitable for young ladies."

"Nothing of the sort!" Max said, ignoring the look of dismay that was spreading over George's face once again. Then, as his young cousin was searching for words, apparently ready to argue the point despite all feelings of duty and familial respect, he continued. "You, George, will drive Miss St. Wilfred in that pony cart that I saw this morning behind the stables. And the rest of us shall ride. Even canter. And stop that poppycock about a decorous pace, will you? This is not Hyde Park."

Relieved and more than a little abashed, George nodded his agreement to this plan and hurried to put it into effect. Fortunately, no one was paying any attention to Mr. Gascoigne's expression, or they might have been shocked. Soon, all was ready.

At Daphne's insistence, they took a little used lane generally reserved for farm wagons, one that carried them straight to their destination instead of along a winding route that covered an extra two miles. "See, Mr. Gascoigne? I keep my word! We shall soon see the sand and waves!" she teased.

He responded with what charm he could muster. "I am chagrined that I failed so signally to put my trust in you, Miss Daphne. In future, I shall obey you implicitly, follow blindly wherever you lead." He began to sidle his mount closer to hers, for they were still moving at a walk and it was possible to exchange a few private words in low tones. To his exasperation, a gate loomed up. He reined in his stallion, allowing him to paw the ground and snort ferociously. "Now what?"

"I suppose that one of us shall have to climb down and open it," Max said with a grin. Seeing that the other man could do no more than scowl, he began to ease his weight over to his left leg before swinging out of the saddle. A shout from George arrested his motion.

A strange cackling sound could be heard above a thrashing in the underbrush, and after a moment of suspense, a stooped and aged figure appeared. The man, for such was the creature, looked to have slept in the open, for his shabby smock and britches were covered with dirt and leaves and a long twig clung to a curl in the rim of his battered hat.

"Be so good as to open the gate for us, Jed," George called out from the cart. The aged man seemed to take a minute to comprehend this command, then he shambled toward the gate.

"Go ye to the tower?" he croaked as he slowly wrested the gate's latch off its rusty resting place.

103

"We may," Max answered.

Old Jed paused to rest on the unlatched, though still shut, gate, considering this information. Finally he shook his head and said, "Safe enough when there be a sun in the sky."

"Yes, it could be a dangerous ride in the dark, but we needn't fear that," Max agreed, amused by the man's ponderous show of concern.

"The ride be no danger, sur," the old man mumbled into the wisps of his beard.

"We have been that way before and come to no danger, my good man," George protested. "The tower is perfectly safe."

"Ah, by day!"

"Open the gate, you old fool!" Gascoigne rasped, but no one heeded his command, least of all the country-man.

"Then you are saying that there is danger in the tower?" Daphne asked with wide eyes and a hint of a twinkle.

"Danger? A haunt, that do be in the tower." The gate slowly began to swing open and the odd figure pushed against it as if the whole of his weight was needed to make it move.

"You mean to say that the tower is haunted?" Max asked, his voice admirably solemn.

"They do walk at night. About the witching hour," his informer agreed.

"They? Do you mean there is more than one ghost?" Daphne pressed. She had been watching the man closely, studying his face and speech.

Jed stopped to consider this, standing in the middle of the now opened gate. "Hard to say, hard to say. They do flit in a winder and out anudder, you see."

"I thought you said they walked!" Max murmured provocatively.

"That must make it very hard to keep count of them," the girl said with a nod.

"That be sure, missy. They move in and out, way up above the ground. Some say they be monks. Leastwise, some seen long dark robes on they." He nodded sagely, moving slowly to one side to allow them to pass. "Ye be wary of the tower, miss. Heed old Jed. He knows of what he tell."

"I shall," Daphne promised. "And you must remember to warn my brother about it, too."

"Eh?" The stooped figure had halted again, leaving the gate untouched although the party had now passed through."

"My brother, Willie. He has spent some time with you, I collect. At least, I saw the two of you talking with one another this week past, out near the stile into the upper fields."

He glared at her, then nodded his head. "Aye. You do mean the young master. I warned him, too. Wouldn't do for the lad to come to harm up there on the cliff. That place be a trap to catch 'un."

"It is not a trap, it is a bell tower," George said with irritation clear in his voice. "Of Saxon-making, a fine example . . ."

"Of clunch," his cousin finished for him. "Now, we must hurry and catch up with Mr. Gascoigne. He seems to have forged a trail for us by galloping on ahead."

Old Jed had the last word as he pocketed the coin tossed to him by George. "Beware the haunt! It'll do you harm. Beware the tower!"

11.

Daphne's hopes for that afternoon's ride were sadly deflated. After spending the whole of the afternoon squiring Emily about in the most protective and attentive way imaginable, George had failed to come up to scratch! The more she considered it, Daphne was forced to question just how much good the outing had done.

It would seem very little. Emily with her foolish fear of horses, although how anyone could be nervous of such dear, sweet creatures she could not understand!, had nearly ruined it all. Her obvious unwillingness to ride any further than Wade Hall had aroused George's protective instincts, which was all to the good, but it had almost meant that the ride was called off, thus losing an opportunity for Emily and George to be alone. If it hadn't been for Max's truly masterful suggestion that George drive her in the dog cart, the whole day would have been a loss! Instead, it had placed the courting couple, for so Daphne insisted to herself they were, in the closest proximity to one another, and all in a perfectly unexceptional manner. Thanks to Max this much had been salvaged from what promised to be a total disaster. The tête-à-tête for the two was more than she could have hoped for.

But what good had it done? For all his masterful concern for Emily's well being, his protective stance when he saw she was afraid to get back on her mount, he had *not* declared himself! What good was a strong masculine arm to lean on if you weren't married to it? It would slip away just when you needed it most. And it was especially devastating if you really wanted to marry the man, were in fact in love with him. Daphne sadly feared that the afternoon's events had made her sister even more unhappy.

She paused to consider this last thought. She was sure that Emily loved George. Or she thought she was sure. True, there were no indications of a grand passion such as she read of in certain romantic novels. Emily didn't sigh or have dreams about him or faint, except over the mouse, of course. But Emily had never indulged in that sort of display. No, Emily would express herself with quiet devotion, ready understanding, warmth and trust. As nearly as Daphne could tell, that described to perfection her sister's attitude toward George, without there being much for an observer to interpret.

But George, who had had several marvelous opportunities to get to know Emily and fall in love with her, and even propose to her, had thrown them all away. The day in the music room had been exciting and touching and terribly romantic, just like in a book, but he had merely chafed the fainted girl's hand, not pressed reviving kisses to her lips. Perhaps the presence of Mama and Papa had abashed him then, but they had been alone for nearly an hour during the picnic, and again, no declaration. Daphne was willing to wager all her pin money for the coming quarter that there had not even been a kiss exchanged. Then there was the trip to the church tower, tea with Lady Forbisher, the maze, the dog cart ride. . . . No, George was a terrible disappointment.

But Daphne being Daphne was not going to let mere disappointment deflect her from the goal she had set.

"George!"

It was Sunday, the service of morning prayer had just ended, and the congregation of the private chapel at the Close was released for another week. Daphne's voice cut across the damp air as she saw her prey sneaking away toward his horse. His retreat detected, George Wade-Hambledon turned to face his young neighbor as courtesy demanded.

"Daphne? Has something happened?" His voice was unusually gruff, a surprising hint of discomposure in a man who was phlegmatic to the point of dullness.

"Happened? Why, not a thing." She smiled up at

109

him artfully, slipping her hand into the crook of his elbow. Firmly captured, George had no recourse but to follow her along the path toward the kitchen garden. "I just wanted to have a little chat with you, that's all."

"A chat?" He frowned over the word. "Do you mean you wish to discuss something with me? Whatever can that be?"

Daphne bit her lip with irritation, then smiled again, stifling her rebellious thoughts. How could he be so ungallant? "I wasn't aware that there need be more reason than friendship, George, for two people to enjoy a friendly talk. We are friends, aren't we?"

"Of course. We've known one another all of your life, so to speak. At least, I have been in the neighborhood that long. But it's drizzling now, and in an hour or so it will be raining in torrents. If I don't leave for the Hall immediately, I shall get caught in the downpour, dash it!"

"Nonsense! It's clearing right now. I can tell."

He stared at her with as close an approximation of exasperation as he would allow himself, then bowed stiffly and waited for her next comment.

"It's just that I so rely on you, George. You set an example for me, with your elevated thoughts and your fine sensibilities! You must not make a stranger of yourself."

"I have visited the Close every day for the past week, Daphne. You've had plenty of opportunity to see me!" He was beginning to sound mutinous, even rude.

110

"Yes, well . . ." Hesitating, she saw that it was futile to try to rationalize her sudden desire to talk with George. He wasn't going to be satisfied with any of her madeup explanations, and he would be horrified if he knew the real reason for her interest. After all, her attention was unprecedented. She decided to ignore his question. "It has been a lovely week, hasn't it? So many things to do, and the excitement of visitors. I do so like your cousin Max, Lord Edenbury, I should say. He is a most charming and amiable companion." Without knowing how, she had suddenly caught his attention.

"Yes, my cousin is the perfect gentleman. He has been extraordinarily good to me, and I am enormously fond of him. I seek only his happiness. It grieves me that he has no wife and family to make his life complete." He watched her closely from the corner of his eye, trying to judge her reaction without seeming to.

"I particularly enjoyed our visit to the church tower," she prattled on, determined to follow her own line of chitchat no matter what tangents George offered.

"You and Edenbury were able to spend a considerable amount of time together that day, as I recall."

"I suppose so. But it was you and Emily who particularly caught my fancy! What a handsome picture you made, standing there on the stairs of the tower, the sun streaming in on you. A very handsome *couple,* that was my very first thought as I watched you together. And the way you were instructing her, so gently, so, so . . ." She had entangled herself in her own rhetoric.

111

It didn't seem to make any difference. George wasn't paying any heed to what she said. "I know for a fact that my cousin, although at times he may appear to be a trifle austere, has the warmest regard for you, Daphne. I trust that you and he have every opportunity to become better acquainted with one another . . ."

She cut in ruthlessly. "I always find churches so romantic, don't you, George? Even if they are for the most part tumbled down. There is something about them that leads my mind inexorably to weddings. What do you think of that, George?"

He beamed with pleasure. "It is but the natural fancy of a young lady looking forward to her own marriage. You are fast approaching an age when such things should be considered, and I am pleased that your thoughts should be so proper, Daphne. I detect in you none of this modern determination to frivol away your time on endless Seasons. Not that you shouldn't have your time in London, but it shows that you are remarkably sensible, to have your heart set on marriage." He was actually patting her hand.

"Emily feels the same way about churches and marriage that I do, George."

"I am pleased that this is so."

"George, how do you feel about the church?" She turned to look him squarely in the eye.

"The Church?" For a moment his usually satisfied expression crumbled, and she was sure that she detected dismay on his face. "How did you know? There was surely nothing I have said or done. . . ." Realizing that he had in fact said quite a lot, George let his words die on their own accord.

"Doesn't the old church make you think of weddings?" Daphne asked, perplexed.

"The old church?" The pompous mask had slipped back into place, and he stared at her with what she thought was a hint of irritation. "You've been talking about the old ruined church?"

"Yes, of course. What's wrong with that?"

"Of all the foolish starts! Daphne, I can't imagine what you've taken into your head to believe about that old ruin, but you must heed my advice and dismiss it from your mind," he ordered austerely.

She glared at him for a moment, then her eyes narrowed. "I can think of no reason why I should ignore the ruin. It is most romantic. Especially the tower."

"The tower is undoubtedly very dangerous, and you must promise me that you will not go back there, not ever again. It was very foolish of us to have explored it as we did the other afternoon. You must forget all about it."

"What can be disreputable about the church?" she asked in a tone that was heavy with accusation.

"I did not say disreputable. And I do not wish to discuss this any further!" he snapped. "And if I do not leave for the Hall on the instant, I shall be drenched in a downpour, I feel certain."

"Piffle."

He raised his chin and pulled himself up to his full height, the better to abash her. "Good day to you."

By the time Daphne had found her way back to her room, it had begun to rain in earnest. It made no difference to her. There was something definitely, distinctly odd about George and the way he was talking about the church and its tower. He was trying to hide something from her, of that she was sure.

But what? Whatever it could be, it must have something to do with the ruin. Why else should he try to dissuade her from exploring it again? True, she recalled seeing nothing of a suspicious nature on their group foray into it, only that it was in better repair than she recollected from her visit last summer. It was almost as if someone was putting the old tower to use, fixing it up for that end. And that someone didn't want anyone to be aware of the activity.

Yes, George definitely had some secret to hide that concerned the church, and she hadn't far to look for the answer to her question.

A tall tower, in an isolated situation, with an unimpeded view of the coastline could be put to only one use she knew of. Smuggling. She remembered the stories she had heard from time to time, stories becoming scarcer as the Gentlemen put aside their Trade or were frightened away from it by the government's patrols. Somehow, someone was using the tower as a lookout for the smuggling enterprise. They had effected repairs on the interior for their convenience. It wouldn't do for the man standing watch to fall on the stairs and hurt himself. Yes, that must be what the mystery was all about!

And George, dear, stuffy, proper George, was somehow involved. And desperately anxious that she stay away from the scene of his activities and whatever clues might be hidden there. George was a smuggler!

She couldn't imagine how or why he should take up such an activity, she had always assumed him to have a comfortable fortune. But one never knew. She shook her head in worldweary disillusionment. And this was the man with whom sweet, innocent Emily had fallen in love! The man she wished to marry! What was Daphne to do? She must stop it. But could she?

Her resolve was formed on the instant. She would make it possible for Emily to have her happiness, and her respectability. Emily would marry George, and Daphne would let this happen with a clear conscience, because George was going to be weaned from his associations with those smugglers. Daphne would see to that!

Just how she would go about it she wasn't sure. She couldn't seek assistance, not even advice, for she would have to tell what she knew, and at all costs word must not get out. Vaguely, she thought she would try to find out more, seek proof with which to confront the villain, proof that would convince him he must give up his way of life or be exposed, come what may. Proof that would reform him. And it was all so thoroughly exasperating! How could George have done such a thing?

The thought of him riding home in the rain, soaked, was the only satisfaction she could find.

12.

Daphne's resolve of silence was nearly shaken Monday morning when Max appeared at the Close.

"Well, I've come for a consultation, Daphy," he announced as he flung himself on to the garden bench facing the music room window.

"Consultation?" she asked with alarm.

"Of course." Catching the tone of her voice, he looked at her sharply. "I noticed that you kept old George with you after church service yesterday, and I was wondering what you were up to."

Relief flooded over her. For one panic-stricken moment, she had thought that he'd guessed George's secret. Here was someone she could turn to for advice, someone with authority over George, enough to make him heed a warning and quit his nefarious enterprise, someone with a knowledge of the world who would know how to keep Emily's lover out of trouble. And someone who would be deeply hurt if he knew the whole of the truth.

"Our campaign, you know. I thought you were up to some more matchmaking yesterday." He added with a smile, "You haven't been impetuous, have you?"

"Impetuous? I?" She gasped for breath. "What did George say?"

"Only that he didn't think you should spend your time about the tower, not that you would, in any case. And he grumbled that he'd gotten wet through because of you. He was positively fraternal in his concern. Isn't that a good sign?"

Her heart beat faster. "I don't see why it should be." She couldn't say more. What if she somehow gave away the whole of the sordid story?

"Come, come," he said with a laugh. "You do want him for a brother, don't you? He would be if he married Emily, you know."

"Of course, I know. Silly of me." But she really wasn't paying him much attention. The tower, it must all hinge on the tower. Somehow she must discover what it was, that was so important she must not be allowed to discover it.

"Well, I had thought you might have said something out of the ordinary to George, which would never do, but I gather I have misjudged you sadly. Your talk with him must have been quite unexceptional. In fact, aside from the tower, he seemed rather pleased. Whatever did you say to him?"

Unexceptional? Pleased? "Only that I wasn't to go into the tower," she answered bitterly. He must have thought that I would obey him blindly, she thought to herself. Well, George had a big surprise in store if he really believed she was as poor-spirited as that. She'd show him!

"But what did *you* say?"

There was a note of suspicion in his voice and she glanced up with surprise to find him staring at her intently. "Oh, very little. I was just gossiping with him about our jaunts during the last few days."

"Oh?" Now he plainly disbelieved her.

Daphne stared at him in dismay. She must be more careful than this if she was to keep the secret! Under no circumstances should Max know that his cousin, his closest kinsman, was an outlaw, a criminal who flaunted His Majesty's laws, smuggling goods in from the Continent. As she thought of those jaunts across the Channel, it occurred to her that George must have been trafficking with the French. Was he a traitor, too? He could well be.

No, Max must not be told of this dishonor. He might feel compelled to surrender George to the authorities, and that would never do. And he would certainly feel hurt and humiliated that such a scandal should fester in his own family, that his cousin was a viper at his breast. Max must never know and she must do a better job of keeping her secret.

But what to say? Then his own hints and suspicions regarding her possible indiscretion gave her a clue.

"I did just mention how romantic churches are, even

119

ruined ones, and how it made one think of weddings."

Suddenly, he was laughing. "Daphy, how could you? I should have guessed!"

"Well, he didn't seem to mind. In fact, he said it was very proper of me to feel that way. And I told him that Emily does, too, although I'm not altogether sure that she does, but it was a good chance to bring her into the talk, and he said that that was as it should be. He seemed positively cheerful when we talked about marriage." She ended on a note of resentment that Max misinterpreted.

"But he still hasn't made a move, eh? Well, never fear, it will come. He just likes to take his time."

Daphne, her mind on George's unscrupulous cunning which had kept the conversation away from the tower and moved it to other, safer topics, nearly stamped her foot. The tower was what counted with him, that was obvious, weddings were but a safe topic for diverting her. She would see about that!

"You must be patient," Max added, seeing her scowl. "Daphne, dear, if worse comes to worse, I shall speak to him myself. It would be fitting enough, if he still seems to be interested in Emily after a month or two. After all, I do have some reason to express an interest in the matter, he's my heir. And it would be more fitting if I spoke, as head of the family and his closest relative, than for you, Emily's younger sister. Is that plan fair enough?"

She failed to answer, perhaps she hadn't even heard him, much to his distress.

"Daphne, don't be so downcast. I promise you that it

120

will all turn out as you wish. It's as important to me as it is to you," he said, the last spoken under his breath.

Shaking herself, the girl came out of her reverie. Whatever she might do about George, she must wait until she could do it alone. And in the interim, there was Max to be dealt with.

"It's very sweet of you to offer, I'm sure," she said at random, having caught only the general import of his statement and not its intensity.

"Yes, that's very well." It was curiously deflating to have her be so casual about his offer, and Max struggled for words. Today the conversational burden was firmly on his shoulders. "I wanted to discuss with you our idea for a costume ball, Daphne. You remember that we thought about arranging one, don't you? As a means of throwing George and Emily together?"

She smiled. "Yes, of course. A ball." Then she realized that it would be her very first ball, and her face lit up. "It would be just the thing!"

He sighed with relief. "I thought so, too."

"They can dress as a pair of lovers from history. Romeo and Juliet, perhaps?"

"Romeo? I can't envisage George climbing balconies. Nor sporting tights."

She chuckled with him. "No more can I. And Emily would never consent to taking poison, or doing anything so improper as to marry without Papa's approval."

"Anthony and Cleopatra?"

"A noble Roman! Just the thing for George. But Emily as Cleopatra? I'm not sure that that would do."

"Well, we shall think more on it later. It needn't be a Shakespearian couple, after all."

She was fairly glowing at him now. "This may be just the thing to bring George about. I was never so disappointed as when he failed to come up to scratch in the gig!"

"Yes, well, there was company about," Max pointed out with a smile.

"Still, it was very clever of you to suggest it! *I* never would have thought of the dog cart," she said handsomely.

"I'm glad I've pleased you."

"Perhaps you should have arranged for the horse to bolt with them! That would have been terribly romantic. And George would have been quite a hero."

"That sounds rather too drastic to me, Daphne. Besides, I don't think George needs to be a hero in Emily's eyes. Let's turn our attention to the party."

"Mama must be asked, and a date set!"

"And you must plan the food and entertainment and the guest list and decorations for the rooms and all sorts of things," he added. His grin widened as he saw her mounting dismay.

"I hadn't thought of all that! There is so much work that goes into a party, isn't there?"

"Yes, there is. And you must do your fair share of it. After all, it's our idea."

"What of you?" she demanded.

"I fear that I'm residing in the wrong household to be of much help. And planning parties is a feminine job, in any case!"

122

"Piffle!"

"You shall be very busy for the next few days, I'm sure."

Daphne, remembering again her own secret plans, stopped when she heard this reminder. What was she going to do, she wondered worriedly. But before Max could notice her abrupt change in mood, they were interrupted.

"Lord Edenbury, sir, you are just the person I've been looking for," young Willie said in an earnest voice as he stumbled through the music room window into the garden, carrying a large volume in his hands and staggering slightly under its weight.

"Willie, mind your manners!" Daphne said automatically.

"Beg pardon, sir, m'lord," the boy said with a slight bow made awkward by the book. "But I know that *you* will be vastly interested in this." He thrust out the volume.

"Interested in a dusty old book? Come, now, Willie," his sister scolded. "I'm sure his lordship has better things to do."

"Now, Daphne, you must let me judge for myself," Max said with a laugh. "Just what is it?"

"It is not a dusty old book, it is a new, clean one that has only just arrived. Sym the carter brought it up from the village with a load of sacking and barrels."

"Sym brought it? And you said your book was clean. I bet it smells even worse than his cart!"

"Let me just glance at it," Max said as he saw the brother and sister preparing to square off.

As he was relinquishing the heavy tome, Willie explained, "I recollected your interest in astronomy as soon as I saw that this book had arrived. We discussed it at table the first time we met. Do you recall?"

Max nodded his head, for he did have some vague memories of the boy's enthusiasm for the stars and planets. "I'm afraid that I know very little about it, Willie," he said.

"Then I shall explain it to you! As best I can. If you'd like to come into the library, I have several more works on the subject. Isn't it fascinating to know that there are stars up in the heavens that we never even guessed existed until the telescope was invented? I hope I'll be able to discover one of my own, some day." He had pulled Max to his feet and was turning to the French windows when the man laughed and protested.

"I was conversing with your sister, Willie. We can't abandon her."

"But it's only Daphy!"

"Well!" Daphne's voice was huffy with indignation. "Only Daphy will carry herself off this instant!"

"Daphne, please don't be offended!" Max begged, stifling an impulse to laugh.

"Well, she can come, too, if you say she must," Willie offered magnanimously. "But girls don't understand these things, you know."

"I'm sure that with your command of the subject, you could explain it so that your sister understood as much as I," Max said soothingly.

"You needn't worry, Willie. I haven't the time to

waste on such foolishness," Daphne said with a toss of her head. "By your leave, sir, I shall set about the preparations for the ball. As you have already explained, there is much to be done." And I might be able to slip up to the tower this afternoon if I'm clever about it, she thought to herself.

Now helpless in Willie's inexorable grip, Max sketched a nod of understanding and farewell, relieved that she appeared to be back to her old self, his earlier concern for her poor spirits fading.

This dispersal was watched from the window of the music room, where Emily and George had been sorting through sheet music together.

"There, did you see? They had some sort of a quarrel!" George pointed out with triumph.

"A quarrel is hardly a propitious clue to the state of their feelings for one another," Emily chided.

"But they aren't indifferent to one another! Max hardly ever bothers with people to the extent of disagreeing with them. He just walks away. It was a lovers' quarrel."

"George!" Seeing her shock and distress over the bluntness of his terms, he was immediately abashed.

"Well, everyone knows that lovers are always quarreling. Isn't that so?"

Emily felt a pang of dismay that had nothing to do with the indelicacy of the word lover. She and George had never had so much as the smallest of disagreements. "If you say so, it must be true, George."

"Then I am right in encouraging this closeness

125

between them. Max will soon see that his feelings for the girl are far different than what he has felt for any other lady. And then he'll marry her!"

"It all sounds so hasty, when you put it like that. Daphne is but a child. She is not even seventeen."

"My grandmother was just that age when she married. Perhaps it is a tradition in the Wade-Hambledon family, although in truth I have not heard of it before. But if it is so, Max will be all the more ready to marry her."

She looked doubtful. "I think he will choose his wife regardless of family traditions."

"But we can't wait!"

"Why is there such urgency? Can't it wait a few months?"

"Max must get married immediately. Before my own plans can be effected." He halted, embarrassed. "I fear that I cannot say more, but I'm sure that you, dear, sweet lady that you are, will trust me and understand. Max must be married, don't you see?"

Emily didn't see, not at all, but she smiled at him sweetly and nodded her agreement, and they turned back to the music.

13.

The path along the cliff was rougher than Daphne had remembered it to be, but she didn't allow this to discourage her. She had wisely chosen to wear her oldest frock, one that was too small for her through the shoulders, but one on which any tears and streaks of mud made no difference.

No, what made a difference was that she approach the tower unseen and unsuspected. She must explore it and find the secret she was sure was hidden there. For the sake of Emily and her future happiness with George, the mystery must be solved. By taking this little-used path, one that hadn't known a human foot since the winter, if the brambles were any proof, she would avoid encountering another person and the explanations and comments such a meeting would entail. And she would be taking a far more direct route, saving time and keeping anyone from noticing her absence.

The sun was shimmering off the water to her right as she reached a high point in the cliffs which gave her a clear view of the sea. She paused to enjoy this, wondering how something so beautiful could create, or at least contribute to, her present predicament. Until now, the sea had always been her friend. For the first time in her life it occurred to her that it might be nice to live inland, far from the coast. Many miles inland. There weren't any smugglers if you went far enough.

Ahead of her, about a half mile distant, the tower rose above the screening undergrowth that choked its base. The tangle of weeds and vines seemed to spill over the cliff to the small beach below, where she could just make out the small boats and piers that were the small harbor of the fishing fleet that trolled these waters. Most of the boats were out in the Channel, discernible on the horizon, but there were the smaller crafts about that one always found in a harbor, no matter how humble, still tied to the docks or anchored near shore.

A seagull laughing overhead broke her reverie, reminding her that she had no time to waste. With a sigh, she heaved herself to her feet and pushed through yet another tangle of bristling thorn bushes. She suffered yet another scratch on her elbow and jerked her arm away, muttering crossly. Past that point, her way was easier and in a mere quarter of an hour she had reached the base of the tower. No one seemed to be about.

Pushing open the door, she entered the dusky coolness and mounted the stairs, circling up and up. In a moment she had passed the first of the windows, pausing only a moment at it to assure herself that no one was approaching the edifice. Reassured, she hurried up the rest of the stairs until she was approaching a ladder that led to the remarkably well preserved platform above her head. With a glance up at the trapdoor, she reached for the rungs.

There was only one barrier to her rapid ascent; the many splinters adding their wounds to those of the brambles. At one point half way up, her skirt caught in a nail, and she heard an ominous tear as she pulled herself free. But neither the state of her clothes, the dust and cobwebs streaking her face and hair, nor the drop she would suffer if she slipped and fell, stopped her. A spider scurrying down a silken line swayed just inches from her nose.

To her relief, the trapdoor opened easily to her touch. Whoever kept their secrets here, they didn't expect an invasion of their privacy. Balancing precariously on the ladder, she pushed and shoved until the door swung all the way open and landed with an echoing thud on the floor of the platform above her head. In a trice, steadying herself with the reassuring solidity of the wall, she was off the ladder and onto solid flooring again, able to study her surroundings.

They were in a remarkable state of preservation. Perhaps George was right and this ground was holy, for it was almost a miracle that the platform's wooden planks hadn't rotted away centuries past. It was only her own sure knowledge that as little a time ago as last summer, the floor *had* been full of gaping holes, that convinced her it was human intervention, not divine, that accounted for the solidity of the floor beneath her feet.

She had been out on a ramble along the cliff, accompanied by a child from the village, when they had been overtaken by a sudden thunderstorm. The tower had been the nearest shelter, and in the drenching downpour they made for it without hesitation.

It was after they had reached its shelter that the other youngster, a girl of about twelve, had begun to whimper. The lightning flashes that lit the interior of the circling walls were certainly eerie enough, there was a disconcerting amount of dirt and dust, and they were soaked to the skin, but it was only after the child had started to sob that Daphne discovered the true cause for her discomfort. The tower was rumored to be haunted. A light had been seen flitting about its base and interior several times, always well after the dreaded hour of midnight. Many of the countryfolk were convinced that a ghost, perhaps of some poor soul who should have rested in the weed-infested graveyard nearby, haunted it.

Daphne had laughed at the time, and later been reminded of the tale and amused when the loquacious and slow moving old man had recounted the current superstition, a more extravagant one, as he opened the gate for them in the nearby field. The notion of monks flying through the air, flitting out one window and into another, was certainly more amusing than a simple ghoul rising from the grave and walking. But there had been an intervening winter and plenty of time to elaborate these details around the Cherry Tree's friendly tables.

Daphne had attempted to disprove the ghost theory to the child when first she heard it. As the storm clouds drifted inland and a weak sunlight made its way through the window slits to light the interior, she had tried to explore what was left of the tower. At the time, there had been very little to see. The ceiling overhead that had once separated the bell from the body of the tower, was pocked with treacherous holes, the bell was long since removed, and even the stone steps that had worked their way around the walls of the tower and upward were too crumbled to risk mounting them far past the first window. It was not so now.

The steps had been carefully remortared, then smeared with dirt to present an impression of age. By scraping away the grime she had seen earlier that the cement holding the stones in place was fresh and new, far stronger than any clunch the ancient Saxons might have used. And the platform, with its attendant ladder, was sturdy and whole. Someone had carefully found planks that gave the appearance of weathered age but were still sound, and repaired the floor with them. She was sure that the ladder hadn't been there last summer, neither on the stone landing nor the rough dirt floor down below.

Now that she was in what had been meant as the bell room long ago, she poked around vigorously. But there was surprisingly little to see. Another roof loomed overhead, but it was only partial, allowing glimpses of blue sky to show through, and she could see that the way leading to its trapdoor would put one on very precarious footing indeed, if one were foolish enough to try it. But one corner of the room was well protected, and she gave this shadowy fastness her closest attention. But there seemed to be nothing but sturdy walls under her probing fingers. Her only reward was a view of the Channel beyond.

She nearly gave up, disappointed to the point of tears, her search fruitless. There seemed to be nothing out of the way in the tower's bell chamber, barring its recent repairs, and just to make sure she had thudded and pounded the floor inch by inch, on the off chance of a secret hiding-place between double flooring. But there was nothing. Any hollow sound she heard was too easily attributable to the tower itself, for it was full of echoes. Then she leaned against the window overlooking the sea, breathing in the fresh air and feeling the cool of the breeze on her warm, damp skin, one foot swinging beneath her. It was time to get back to the Close, past time, she thought, and then her foot struck the wall beneath the window and a stone gave way.

Whoever had taken the tower for his hideout, he had not relied on mere wood to hide his secret. A false stone wall hid a small space in the thickness of the tower wall, a space that had perhaps been open there beneath the window when the place was first built. Now the stones had been carefully arranged to shield it from casual eyes. Only the random movement of her foot had moved the keystone that wedged the rest of the false structure together.

She removed the stones quickly, humming under her breath in her excitement, trying not to cause too great a disarray among them. Then there was space enough to thrust one hand in and feel about. And after brushing away spiders and their webs, her fingers encountered something wooden. A box! The rest of the stones fell under her eager hands.

In a moment the box was out on the platform floor, sitting in a shaft of sunlight, waiting for her to discover what lay in it. It was an odd shape, long and narrow, just right for its hiding-place beneath the slit in the wall. Dubious, she turned it over in her hands. Whatever could be hidden away in it? Surely not a treasure! Such boxes were more square, less elongated. And they weighed more. Weapons? They wouldn't fit, at least not any sort she had ever seen. It was too short to hold a musket and not wide enough for more than a brace of hand pistols, which would hardly be worth the effort someone had taken to hide it away. Then her curiosity suffered a check.

The box was locked.

She tried shaking it, poking a stick through the lock, then a hairpin, to no avail. The stone she used to strike it open merely crumbled in her hand. There was nothing more to it: she couldn't get it opened. The box would keep its secrets.

Slowly, almost in tears from frustration, she returned the container to its hiding-place and began to replace the stones. It wouldn't do for whoever had left it there to know that it had been discovered. Not yet. She would save that surprise for later. She might need it, and in the meantime she would seek some means of forcing the lock. Working carefully, she rebuilt the hiding wall.

The sun had swung over the top of the tower by the time she was making her way down the ladder. She would be late for dinner, she feared, but that wasn't so unusual. She had wandered far afield before and arrived home behindtimes. Then a sound below caught her attention and she scrambled down the ladder to the window overlooking the path leading to the tower from the village. A rider was approaching on a fast-moving horse.

Her descent down the stairs nearly ended in a fall, but she was casually gazing out of the first and lowest window, seemingly admiring the view, when the man entered the tower.

"Miss Daphne, what a pleasant surprise!" Gascoigne exclaimed as he removed his hat and bowed. "Allow me to assist you in descending those treacherous steps."

He had reached out his hand as he spoke, walking toward her, and she'd begun to take it when she noticed the state of her own. Covered with scratches from her journey through the brambles, then layered heavily with cobwebs and grime, they were hardly the hands of a lady. Her dress, with a long rent in the skirt, was even worse.

"I can't inflict them on you, sir," she said with a laugh as she made her way down the steps unassisted. "As I managed to find my way up these stairs alone, I'll have to go down alone. My hands have acquired an amazing degree of dust and dirt on them." She held them out for his inspection, not missing the sneer that briefly curled his nostrils.

"You have an enterprising spirit, Miss Daphne. May I ask what you have been doing, to acquire such signs of activity?"

"Doing? Just exploring. The tale of the ghosts intrigued me and I thought I might look for some evidence."

"Surely the best time for such an expedition would be late at night. That is when these ghosts are reputed to walk."

"And fly. It was the flying that particularly appealed to me."

"And did you discover anything of interest?"

"Only an unconscionable amount of dirt, it would seem. There were no signs of a hoax, which was what I expected to find."

"You are intrepid! I would never have dreamed of such an investigation."

"Not really. The steps near the top of the tower are too crumbled for me to risk my weight on them," she explained mendaciously. "You can hardly call such caution intrepid."

He glanced up doubtfully, as if weighing this information. "Then if a person as small as you can't climb higher, neither could I, I would guess."

135

"No, don't try it. I nearly fell through a stretch that looked perfectly safe. One minute I was on firm footing, the next I was scrambling back. Is that why you came? To climb the tower?" She had been walking slowly toward the door, praying that he wouldn't spot the ladder in the shadows over their heads.

He stared into her eyes, convinced of the truth of her words by the limpid clarity he found there, and his own arrogant belief that no one could fool him. "Yes, I, too, was entertained by the tale of the ghosts. And I had hoped for a view of the surrounding countryside. This is the highest vantage point in the neighborhood, and I'd looked forward to a panoramic display." He said this last with a rueful laugh as they walked into the sunlight. "I'll have to go elsewhere."

"Try the hill over toward the Burnett place. You can't see the sea as well, but it has a pretty enough view, and it's an easy ride, really quite pleasant," she advised him as she tried to dust herself off. "Well, you must excuse me, I'm late for dinner."

Recollecting his real intentions toward her, he turned about with dismay. "Can't I claim a few more moments of your charming company? I have so wanted to deepen our acquaintanceship into something warmer, Miss Daphne." He was smiling at her with a winsome twinkle in his eye, the sort that had often swayed the ladies in the past.

" 'Fraid not. They'll be wondering what has become of me. Good-bye for now." And before he could frame another protest, she was making her way through the brambles to the path.

14.

"But a masquerade, my dear! Is that really quite the thing?" Sir Wilfred sputtered into his moustaches.

"I think it is more of a dress up party, dearest. There is no hint of impropriety in Daphne's scheme, I assure you. She is far too innocent to suggest anything of that nature. And I don't think she even expects people to wear dominoes, merely come dressed as some figure from history or literature. It is an opportunity to display some cleverness and wit in one's choice."

Sir Wilfred, glaring down at a corner of the rug that his favorite setter had chewed away, was unconvinced. He was surrounded by testimonials to the sobriety and propriety of his character and family: the mellow oak of the old rectory table cluttered with estate papers, a portrait of some long dead baronet hanging over it, the musty smell of the leather-bound volumes accumulated over generations. The only new feature in his study was a set of needlepointed chair cushions executed by his wife and allowed into his sanctum only because he loved her dearly and couldn't bear to hurt her feelings.

"But masks! Everyone knows what sort of license is taken at such gatherings! I won't have any sort of impropriety in my home!" He looked to his ancestor hanging over the table as if seeking support.

"It will be a masquerade in the sense that the guests will be asked to come in costume, but with their faces plain for all to see. It is the anonymity of wearing concealing cloaks and masks that emboldens some to take liberties that go beyond the line of what is pleasing. And these things usually occur only at the public balls, where all sorts of people might gain admittance. I am sure that at a private gathering of our invited guests, people who are old friends of ours, we shall have no reason to fear anything unbecoming."

"A costume party? Dress up?"

"Yes. It is rather childish in its way. It calls to mind some of our winter evenings, and the charades we enjoyed when the children were little and wanted to be entertained with the dresses and garments stored away in the trunks in the attic."

There was a glimmer of a smile under his moustache and she took heart, knowing that she had struck just the right note with him. She hurried to press the advantage.

"Do you recall their delight when they found your

grandmother's presentation dress? The one she wore when first introduced to Court? And that monstrous hat she wore to our wedding? The one with all the plumes and flowers spilling over the edges?"

He had begun to chuckle. "There are still some of my grandfather's pantaloons hidden away some place in that attic, I'm sure. And Uncle Jack's uniform. It would be just the thing . . ." He broke off with a sputter, glaring at her suspiciously.

"And those lovely old dresses, with all their satin and lace, and the fine needlework covering the whole of the skirts and bodices!"

"And the hoops!" He was chuckling again, shaking his head as he enjoyed these memories.

"It would be just the thing for us to wear!"

"The fifteenth baronet appearing as the thirteenth. You know there was nothing to the notion that thirteen was an unlucky number, my dear, not for my grandfather. Far from it. He was a fine man, well respected, and a very successful one." There was a moment's silent tribute to this ancestor's success, for it was he who had established the family's modern fortunes after some centuries of decline. They gazed reverently at his likeness hanging on the wall.

"Of course, dearest. I well remember the honor my father held him in," his wife agreed.

"Which is not to say that I shall allow this party to take place. Whose idea was it to begin with? Daphy's, I suppose."

"I believe that she and Lord Edenbury hit upon the scheme."

There was a long silence.

"Edenbury?"

"Edenbury."

More silence.

"He has been about quite a bit lately."

"He is a charming man and very fine company,"
Lady St. Wilfred murmured.

"A man of rank and substance."

"We are fortunate to have him visiting in the
neighborhood."

"With a nice sense of *ton*," Sir Wilfred muttered
into his moustaches.

"He would lend prestige to any gathering."

Sir Wilfred straightened his back and looked at his
wife square in the eye. "I look forward to the honor of
his presence at this affair," he announced in a firm
voice.

Lady St. Wilfred smiled and squeezed his arm, gently
steering him to the study door.

"I only hope that the moths haven't done any
damage," he added as an afterthought while they made
their way to the ballroom.

In the middle of its floor stood their youngest
daughter, surrounded by minions and piles of clutter.
It would seem that the fine Adams ballroom, the brain
child of the fourteenth baronet, was being redesigned.

"Are these all you can find?" She asked a parlormaid
with dismay. The servant dithered for a moment, then
curtsied and promised to look for more. The bundle in
her arms was placed on an already overburdened table

and she disappeared through the door, dropping another hasty curtsy to Sir Wilfred and his lady.

"I say, Daphy, just what are you about here?" Sir Wilfred asked as he stared about him.

Lady St. Wilfred had advanced to the table. "Daphy, darling, these are my finest sheets! The good linen ones with embroidery that I save for special guests. What are they doing here in the ballroom?"

"I need them for the decorations, Mama. Just see! I shall transform this room into something truly unusual, something romantic and imaginative and . . ."

"Transform the ballroom? Whatever for?" her father demanded.

"But Papa, it's just a ballroom! A plain old room. I want this party to be the finest that has ever been! I thought a tent-like effect, with swaths of . . ." She broke off as she saw the expression on her parent's face darken.

"A plain old room? This room was designed by the finest architect of the last century. Or of any century, for that matter." Sir Wilfred, nothing if not conservative, with more than his share of reverence for the past, waved his arms as if to embrace the whole of the Adams beauty. "It was built by the finest workmen available, brought down from London, some from as far away as Paris. The best artisans in Europe molded the ceiling and cornice! The painting was carried out under Adams' personal direction. The marble for the mantel came from Italy!" He turned as if to seek one more beauty to bring to her attention. "My God!"

"Wilfred!" his wife admonished, to no avail, casting an anxious glance at her dazed daughter.

"She has thrown a sheet over the Naiad. *My* Naiad! I purchased her myself on my Grand Tour and placed her in that niche with my own hands. Unveil her this instant!"

The only person in the room with sufficient presence of mind to fulfill this command was the butler, who snatched away the offending sheet and hid it behind his back. Sir Wilfred approached his treasure slowly, as if fearing some damage had been done, then sighed with relief.

"There. That's better. Now take away all those sheets and things and tidy up a bit." A silence fell on the room, broken only by the softfooted servants as they hastened to obey. Daphne and her mother held their breath as he turned to face them, each wondering how far his anger would go.

"If there is to be any decoration, it will be flowers and plants, as my mother would have done." He shook a finger at his child. "I shall rely on you to see that my wishes are carried out, Daphy. No more sheets!"

"Yes, Papa. I mean, no, Papa," she gasped, curtsying and then hastening to seal the bargain with a kiss before he could change his mind. "I promise."

"Bring in whatever you need from the greenhouse and garden," Lady St. Wilfred said.

"Thank you, I shall."

"And you must recall that this room is one of the finest ornaments of our home!" her father said austerely. "Don't cover it up!"

142

"Yes, Papa."

"It's beautiful in and of itself. It needs no more. You should be proud of it."

"Of course, yes, Papa, I am."

"Well, get back to work. But one more thing! You have several days yet before this party of yours is to take place. Don't put everything in sixes and sevens until you must."

"Oh, I shall! I mean, I shan't!" she promised eagerly, dreaming already of banks and banks of flowers lining the walls and adorning the tables of the room. As her parents left the room, all thoughts of smuggling were far from her mind.

Much later, as he sat in his garden enjoying the evening air with his wife, Sir Wilfred's brought the conversation back to the planned ball.

"You say that Edenbury's encouraged her to set up this ball?"

"So I understand from Daphy."

"Could be a mistake. She's young, might have misunderstood. . . ."

"Perhaps."

"He's not a young man."

"Nearly thirty."

"Still. To be indulging in such fripperies! Surprisin'."

"I think he only seems serious beyond his years because of the responsibilities he has had to bear. They are considerable, and he came to them at an early age."

"You are very likely right, my dear. But still, when

I met him that day George brought him over to see that stock, he seemed above this sort of nonsense."

"Above it? Come now, it is a perfectly unexceptional party. There is nothing to sneer at about it!" his wife protested.

"No, no. It will be great fun, great fun. Only I took Edenbury for a London dandy. Too sophisticated to bother with rustic pleasures. You know his reputation as well as I! What's he finding so amusin' in all this? It's hardly up to snuff by London standards."

"It could be precisely because it is different from London that charms him." She was smiling into her embroidery as she suggested this, well aware of what was attracting Edenbury's attention.

Her husband snorted. "Can't imagine that! Everyone knows that London's the place to kick up your heels."

"Yes, dear."

"And I am sure he told me that day he planned to take his leave the following Friday, when his business was complete. That date is well passed. And he's still here."

"Then it must be for pleasure."

"Maybe he hasn't finished his business," her husband contradicted.

She looked at him with a sudden sharpening of interest. "Yes, dear, that may well be the case. He still has something to see to here. Some very important personal business, unless I miss my guess."

15.

"I am so glad that we shall appear as a group, Daphy, and not just George and I as a couple," Emily explained for the tenth time as she examined the pleasing effect their costumes made in the shimmering light of the Close's entrance hall. Guests were just starting to arrive, arrayed in a variety of conceits from the pedestrian to the inspired, but the company was thin as yet and the young hostesses had time to gossip.

"Yes, well, I can't imagine why you were so shy about being matched with George. You've known him forever."

Emily, more retiring than her younger sister and with a greater instinct for delicacy, blushed. "I fear it would have been thrusting, and well, forward, if I had suggested such an arrangement. It would not be proper for an unmarried girl to appear so in a gentleman's company, for many would take it to be a declaration on her part. That would never do."

"Emily, no one would ever accuse you of wearing your heart on your sleeve!"

"Nor you," the older girl murmured, but the door had opened again and more friends were arriving.

Emily had had serious misgivings when the scheme for their costumes was first broached. As she had said, it would not do to stir comment and speculation among the other guests. But more than that, she kept a close guard on her own thoughts and would never for the world have allowed George to suspect the true state of her feelings for him. She had too much pride to offer all and then suffer rejection, for she greatly feared that George looked upon her as no more than a dear friend and, at the moment, an ally. Yet the frequent visits necessitated by the creation of their matching costumes had been pleasant indeed.

It had been as an ally furthering George's scheme for his cousin's happiness that she had found the courage to dress as Columbine. Daphne had chosen for her sister what she considered to be the premier feminine role in the old pantomime cast. To match her, George was decked out as Harlequin, but even Emily had to admit that he looked little like a dancer. George's only solace when he faced himself in the mirror, he confided to Emily, was that only Columbine was supposed to be able to see him in this ridiculous rig, or so his recollection of the mime went. It was the closest to a joke that Emily had ever heard pass his lips.

But for Harlequin and Columbine, there must also be a Pierrot and Pierrette. Max as the artist-lover, had turned the white flowing sleeves of his costume with the large buttons in a row down the front, into a gown of elegance and grace. He looked every inch the devoted lover, making no effort to hide behind a comic mask. Any clowning done by Lord Edenbury would be performed with condescension, or so thought Emily; he would make few concessions. But perhaps he sought to amuse Daphne with his antics. And Daphy, dressed in matching white with huge green buttons, was every bit his partner. As George had hoped. Fleetingly, Emily wondered that her younger sister, usually so perceptive, had failed to notice this.

It had not been ignored by some of the guests. Lady Forbisher and her nephew were early arrivals, and clashed in earnest debate on just that subject. Their anger mounting, they had retreated into the privacy of the denuded conservatory.

"What am I to think? They are dressed to match. It must signify something!"

"Don't be foolish, Gerard. Wade-Hambledon and Miss St. Wilfred are also a matched couple. Although a more foolish Harlequin I cannot recollect ever seeing. He is too old for her, in any case."

"Perhaps it is but an intrigue to throw dust in everyone's eyes. I tell you, the girl is besotted with one of them! And look, she can't take her eyes off

Wade-Hambledon. It must be he! Look!" Dragging her to the door of the conservatory, he pointed out across the dance floor.

The evening had progressed to the point where the floor was crowded with dancers, and the couples of the harlequinade had joined together in the same set. It was true, Pierrette had eyes only for Harlequin, Columbine looked worried and unhappy, and Pierrot appeared to be ignoring everything but the pattern of the dance.

"She is much taken with him," Lady Forbisher agreed, watching the scene through narrowed eyes. Taking up her large painted fan with a snap, she began fanning her face. With the high mantilla covered comb in her hair, and the fine details of her embroidered Spanish gown, she looked every inch a Spanish aristocrat. Only Gerard knew her well enough to appreciate that there was a will of steel hidden beneath the lace and satin. But he also knew better than to disturb her while she thought, and instead admired his own reflection in the darkened windowpanes of the conservatory.

He saw much to please and reassure him there. He was of the right age for the girl, merely three and twenty. His costume, that of a Viking warrior, played up his fine physique and fair coloring. His features were considered handsome by many, and so he had disdained any thought of gluing an artificial beard over them. As he stood staring, he realized that with his looks there was no need to worry about his success with Miss Daphne St. Wilfred. And improving the whole of his appearance was that indescribable air of Town bronze about him that could be rivaled by no other gentleman present. Well, almost none.

"But are you sure that she feels affection for him?"

"Why else such interest?"

"But he lacks everything a young girl would seek in a lover! Address, charm, a personable face and figure. There is nothing there but worthiness. Who would want that?"

"Can you fathom a young girl's heart?"

"Better than you, it would seem. You are ten times a better suitor than he, Gerard. Stop this foolish doubting. Just look at yourself and compare what you see with Wade-Hambledon! He is stodgy and dull beyond bearing . . ."

"Unless you are interested in church architecture," he injected with a laugh, his spirits rising.

". . . and you are not only handsome and amusing, you bring an air of something new and different into her life. She has known Wade-Hambledon since childhood. How can she resist someone new and romantic and exciting? You are adventure to her!"

He was smiling as he listened, his eyes lingering on his reflection in the polished panes of the glass walls. "Yet her eyes follow him. Curious."

"You shall have no trouble drawing them to you once you put your mind to it. Behave with confidence! There is nothing more deadly to a gentleman's prospects of success than a timid front."

"As long as it is not Edenbury. . . ."

"Don't sulk so! I've already told you that she is far too young to interest him. I doubt that any woman does," she ended spitefully.

They turned to watch the brilliant scene through the doorway, their eyes seeking out once again the people they had been discussing. The set had reformed. Harlequin was puffing into the face of a young Queen Elizabeth who stood across the floor from him, Pierrette had been led to the far side of the room by a middle aged Cavalier. Pierrot had disappeared from the floor and could be glimpsed leaning over a graying head in a small alcove. Over all a brilliant light was cast by the candles in the crystal and gilt chandeliers, magnified by the many fine mirrors on the walls. The mingled fragrances of many flowers filled the air.

"He does seem to be avoiding the ladies this evening," Gascoigne agreed with a sneer in Pierrot's direction.

"And so he is out of it. There must be some other concern about Wade-Hambledon disturbing the girl," Lady Forbisher suggested thoughtfully.

He turned to her with a look of surprised comprehension. "It was being bruited about that he intended to offer for the elder Miss St. Wilfred. But nothing has come of it. Could that be the root of her interest?"

"I should have thought of that! She may well have Emily's well-being in mind, not her own."

"She has displayed much odd behavior regarding that tower, you know. It was almost as if she didn't want me to be there. I think it has something to do with Wade-Hambledon."

"The tower? That pile of rubble on the cliff?"

"I understand that the only two people in the whole of the neighborhood who have any interest or knowledge of the tower are Miss Daphne and Mr. Wade-Hambledon. And his attention has been of a longer duration than hers."

"Could it be a meeting place? No, not that. She is too naive to indulge in such amusements."

Gascoigne turned to her with a slow smile spreading over his face. The blue eyes were alight with pleasure, and as she looked at him her plucked eyebrows rose expectantly.

"I have just been visited with an inspiration such that only the gods could have delivered!"

"The gods? Which ones?"

"Aphrodite and Cupid."

"But of course," she said with a smile.

"And poor Miss Daphy might look to Europa for an example. Wish me luck!"

"You need none!"

As he led his aunt onto the dance floor, Gascoigne began to consider just what he would do with Daphne's fortune.

16.

Daphne stood near the open French windows, the light breeze from the garden ruffling her skirts unheeded. From there she commanded a view of the whole of the ballroom and not a small portion of the supper room, and she used it to watch George Wade-Hambledon.

Not that George was doing anything to arouse her interest. Rather, he was performing his usual commonplace habits such as one expects of a gentleman attending a social function that on the whole he would rather have avoided. He kept himself well fortified with cups of champagne punch, danced only when forced to do so by his hostess, his two dances with Emily having already been enjoyed, and discussed farming matters and politics with the other gentlemen. In fact, he looked so commonplace, acted so commonplace, was so commonplace, that Daphne found it hard to entertain any suspicions against him.

But perhaps it was all just an elaborate charade, a real life masquerade that concealed his true personality and character. A shield behind which he hid his secret! For Daphne was positive that he had a secret, the mask had slipped often enough that she felt she could be sure. And it all had something to do with that old church and its tower.

She felt a little guilty that she had put it from her mind for so long, but now that the excitement of her first grown-up ball was beginning to wane, she returned to it with determination.

What was the case against George? To begin with, there was his curious reserve toward Emily. Although showing every sign of being deeply in love with the girl, and was of an eligible age and station in life to propose to her, he had maintained the role of devoted family friend. This failed to conceal the warmth of his regard for Emily, the ease of their conversation, the fact that they were in every way suitable for one another. Yet George had not yet adopted the role of suitor. He had not come up to scratch. Could it be that he feared his cousin's disapproval? If so, he was being absurd. Max demonstrated only approval of Emily, even displaying a brotherly affection on occasion. Not even George would be so foolish as to miss that.

Then there was his curious knowledge of the old church tower. For a casual observer, he displayed considerable interest in its construction and history, an interest unusual in a gentleman of his rank. Was it he who had made those repairs to the interior, repairs making the platform of the bell chamber usable? It was an ideal lookout post for someone conducting clandestine activities along the coast, providing a spectacular view up and down the shoreline and well out to sea. And when she had pointed this out, George had shown considerable distress, arguing that the ground was holy, sanctified, and therefore exempt from smugglers' interest. This too was absurd, even fatuous, for worldly men didn't let little things like that stop them. A case in point was her own home, once an abbey, then inhabited by generations of her family, including women of whom the early monks would most certainly have disapproved. George might as well insist that the St. Wilfreds should be turned out of their home, lock, stock and barrel, or that they should never have settled there in the first place.

Since their walk to the village and the visit they had paid the tower, every time she had so much as mentioned the word church George had jumped. Yes, something was seriously amiss.

It was well that most of the guests present were so occupied with their enjoyment that they failed to notice the expression on Daphne's face. It would have raised considerable comment, even amusement. The predictable exception to this was Gerard Gascoigne, who was intrigued by the scowls she was sending in Wade-Hambledon's direction.

He had been toying with plans to guarantee his marriage to the girl, plans that would negate any parental opposition or delay, for he could not afford even a few months of waiting to lay his hands on her money, so serious was his financial position. During his conversation with his aunt, his resolve had hardened. If the girl proved unwilling, his notion of eloping over the border could as easily be transformed into a kidnapping scheme, although he was sure that his charm would win in the end, making that unnecessary. It had now occurred to him that none of this was needed: he had only to compromise the girl, get her away from her family and friends for the length of one night, and she would have no choice but to marry him. And his course lay open before him, lit with marvelous clarity.

"Miss Daphne, might I speak to you alone for a moment?" he murmured from behind her.

Daphne, who had not heard him approaching, spun around, startled. "Whatever do you mean by creeping up on me like that, sir?" Then realizing that she had not been gracious, she added, "You have startled me. I had not seen you so near."

"Please accept my apologies. It was only that I have come with the direst information, and know not to whom to present it, that I have been so clumsy as to approach you in this fashion. I had hoped not to attract any attention ..." Here he hesitated, throwing an artful glance over her shoulder toward the ball-room.

"Attract attention? What is there to hide, sir?" she asked coolly.

He only smiled and shook his head, unruffled by her tone. Then he nodded toward the far corner of the room. She turned to follow his glance.

A merry group of gentlemen were gathered near the punch bowl, some to fetch refreshment for the ladies, others to indulge themselves. Her father must have just delivered a joke, for the group laughed uproariously and there was much backslapping and headshaking. Even George Wade-Hambledon had found it amusing enough to draw a smile. Then the group broke up and went its several ways, and George strode toward the door to the supper room.

Daphne turned back to Gascoigne and saw that his eyes were still following the other man's progress into the adjoining room. His face was bland, only a slight frown puckering his brows.

"I'm afraid, Miss Daphne, very much afraid, that what I must say to you is of an extremely delicate nature. It regards, if I may be so bold as to say so, the activities of a close friend of your family, a man who has enjoyed the greatest intimacy with the St. Wilfreds over the years. I cannot bring myself to believe that there isn't some innocent explanation for what I have seen, but . . ." Now the pucker was furrowing into a frown, and his pale eyes glinted in the direction of the supper room.

"What is this all about, Mr. Gascoigne? Please explain yourself!"

"Explain? I would if I could. But there may be some simple, entirely innocent reason for what Mr. Wade— or rather, the gentleman—has done, but I, in my ignorance as a stranger to the district, am not able to discern it." He shook his head sadly.

"What has he done?" Daphne was now twisting her

handkerchief into a damp rope in her fingers, her anxiety giving her voice a shrill pitch.

He appeared to be startled, then looked at her as if seeing her for the first time. "Forgive me," he murmured. "I should never have approached you on this matter, Miss Daphne. You are too young to be burdened with so adult a concern. Please forget that I said anything, anything at all. We shall let fate plot the course of justice. I'm sure that the gentleman, and those dear to him, will come to no harm."

He turned as if to leave her, but she took a firm grip on his arm and pulled him closer to the open doors. "You must tell me! I've already had my suspicions, but if you *know*, have some evidence, I beg you to place it in my hands. At least tell me what it is!"

He faced her with a look of such sympathy and concern that she was convinced of his sincerity. "It is more suitable that a man, preferably a gentleman of substance and experience, deal with the matter. I could approach his cousin, or perhaps your father would be a better choice, for he has served as a magistrate in these parts, I apprehend. Yes, a magistrate would be the man to inform."

Daphne fought the rising panic that was nearly overwhelming her ability to think and speak. Oh, whatever had George done? And what would become of poor Emily? She must learn more.

"I plead with you, do not act in haste. As you have already said, there may be some innocent explanation for what has happened. Perhaps if I only knew more, I could supply it."

His expression became even more solemn as he gazed down into her pleading eyes. "Dearest child, you are a good and true friend to this man. You're far more trusting than he deserves. Pray, put all that I've said from your mind."

"It would be cruel to ruin a gentleman's reputation without good cause. Even casual talk, later disproved, would be a crushing blow to a gentleman. George is so terribly sensitive about his good name, ridiculously so! He would feel the disgrace in merely being suspected, let alone accused, of something as dreadful as smuggling. Please, let us try to resolve this question quietly, in private, without allowing any others to even guess that there is something wrong."

She held her breath, praying to see what his response would be, praying that she had convinced him. From the look of surprise on his face, she feared she had failed. Then, after a moment or two of consideration, he smiled and patted the hand that still clung to his sleeve.

"So it shall be, Miss Daphne. For the regard I bear you, I shall tell you what little I know."

"Then tell me quickly, please. I cannot bear to wait! I have wondered and worried for so long."

"Shush, you must not speak so. You have said it yourself, we must be careful that no one but the two of us hears our conversation. This is neither the time nor the place for a talk such as we must have."

She glanced about them. It was true, they were surrounded by a crowd of people, any one of whom might approach them without warning. Their few moments of privacy here by the doors had been due to good fortune. Then she tugged at his sleeve.

"The garden! We can talk there. If anyone asks, we were simply seeking a breath of fresh air, enjoying a stroll together. Whatever couples do."

He hid a grin at this last comment and the remarkable naiveté it displayed, then shook his head. "It would be even more dangerous to talk outside in the dark. Someone might happen along without our seeing them and catch us unawares. You must bear the suspense a bit longer. Perhaps tomorrow—"

"Tomorrow? Oh, I cannot wait that long!"

"Then this evening," he said with an air of sudden decision. "After the supper has been served and eaten, it will be easy enough for you to slip away for a rendezvous at someplace where no one can overhear us. Agreed?"

Daphne, relieved that she had carried her point, nodded her head. "Agreed."

"Then we shall meet at the old tower overlooking the sea." He got no further for the moment, so startled was she with this hint of his knowledge.

"Surely you must know all!"

"Not all, dearest maid," he smirked. "Be there an hour after the dancing resumes."

"So late?"

"If you leave now and fail to appear for the meal, it might well attract comment." She had to nod at this. "You will be able to find your way to the tower without mishap?"

"I think so."

160

"I would escort you myself, but that might excite attention. There is a half moon to light your way."

"I'll take the path along the cliff. It will be easy enough."

"Very good. And I shall make my way there on horseback, leaving the party early. We shall be approaching from different directions so no one will suspect anything."

She was still frowning slightly and he cast a sharp glance her way, only to be reassured when she nodded her head again. "It's the only way. I must know what is happening as soon as possible, if I am to straighten out this mess."

He took her hand and squeezed it. "You're a very brave young lady."

"I don't know about that. But something must be done, surely you can see that! And there seems to be no one else about to take care of the problem, so it's up to me."

"And me."

"Well, yes, thank you very much, but . . ."

"Please don't deny me this opportunity to do you some service, to express my feelings for you in actions rather than words. Let me prove myself!"

She looked straight into his eyes, noting their pale, unattractive glistening and shrugged. "I suppose I shall rely on you for some assistance. But I can hardly promise you until I know what I'm going to do."

"Of course, I apprehend perfectly."

But she wasn't listening. "If you want something done, you just have to do it yourself," she sighed.

17.

Daphne approached the tower just as the clouds broke to reveal a sliver of moon hovering in the air above the crumbling ruins. Its faint rays played with the bushes and uneven walls, casting eerie splashes of black and silver that seemed to dance and sway across the landscape. She felt herself shiver, and then firmly ignored it. There was nothing to be afraid of. There were no such things as ghosts, the tower wasn't haunted, except perhaps by real, live smugglers. She hurried up the path, grumbling under her breath at the delays she had suffered in setting out, her maid's obstinacy, the brambles that got in her way, as if this were a commonplace outing. In her heart she longed for sunshine and company.

The uneven door to the edifice was in deep shadow

and she hesitated before it a moment, imagining she heard something else within, some noise she was unable to identify. The moon was now occasionally in view, then again hidden by the scurrying clouds. Lights winked on and off in the Channel, reminding her of her isolation.

"Mr. Gascoigne, is that you? Have you arrived already?" she called out.

Only a faint rustling of the bushes answered. A night animal, she told herself as she reached the door. Peeking into the gloom, she was uncertain as to whether she should wait for the gentleman inside or without. To her surprise, she saw that the upper portion of the tower's interior was quite bright, slashed by milky moonlight playing on the walls. Dust particles in the air reflected the light in a hazy glow. Reassured, she stepped through the door, each move taken slowly and with care, and looked around her.

There was nothing to be afraid of. Nothing had changed from her previous visit, nothing been removed, nothing added. There was just the dusty, crumbling lower room of the tower, its only contents the rubble of sticks and pebbles from the decaying walls lying scattered about on the floor.

There was a faint scraping sound and Daphne jumped, panicked but unsure where the danger lay. The sound seemed to echo through the room and she could not pinpoint whatever had made it. It might be hovering outside, waiting for her to leave, ready to capture her when she fled this sanctuary. What to do? Hide in here from the outside danger? But what if the danger were *in* and not *out?* She shivered uncontrollably, pressing her back against the wall, trying to convince herself that it had been only a rat scurrying home through the bushes.

The sound of a horse threw her into further turmoil, but a glance though the door showed that its rider was approaching the tower openly, as if he had nothing to hide. A closer look revealed that the newcomer was Gerard Gascoigne, not a smuggler.

"Mr. Gascoigne!" she gasped as she hurried outside. "I had thought you would never come!"

"Forgive me, dear Miss Daphne, but the way was unfamiliar to me and I traveled slowly for fear of losing myself or laming the horse. Has something happened to frighten you?" He smiled to himself, for if so, it suited his plans well enough. A few moments alone in the darkened tower would go far to weaken the strongest spirit.

"Yes, I mean, no, I mean— It is just that there are all sorts of noises, and everything looks very different in the moonlight."

He looked down at her with a quirky twist of his mouth that told her of his amusement at her expense. "You, my dear Miss Daphne, look even more ravishing by moonlight than you do by candlelight," he said as he dismounted, ignoring her earlier plight.

He had come to stand directly before her, so close that she took a step back involuntarily. "That's not the point. You have said you know something about George Wade-Hambledon. Something of vital importance."

"Something to his discredit," Gascoigne said with a chuckle, taking another step toward her.

"Be that as it may, you have promised to tell me what you know. All of it."

"I shall be more than glad to tell you all, my dear. But first, shouldn't we step into the tower, so that we shall be out of view if a casual passerby should happen in the neighborhood?"

"Who would be wandering about here at this hour?" she asked, then added, relenting, "Oh, very well. We shall talk inside."

"It's so very much more private there."

They were soon standing in the thick reflecting light of the tower's lower chamber, Daphne keeping her distance as best she could, her back toward the steps.

"Well? What is your news?"

"My news is that I love you!" he said in a soft, husky voice, stepping closer to her.

"Piffle. You say that to everyone, I should imagine. I came to hear about George."

"Why should you care about a dull dog such as he is beyond me!" His exasperation renewed the usual sharp edge to his voice.

"He's in trouble, as you well know, and I'm going to get him out of it if it's the last thing I do!"

"Why bother? Are you in love with him?"

"No! Of course not! My sister Emily is. But that's neither here nor there."

"So you have dreamed up some loathsome crime for poor, dull George to have committed? How romantic!

166

Just what is he supposed to have done? Pilfer the church alms-box? That seems most likely, he spends so much time on his knees."

"Pilfer? Then you don't know about the smuggling?" She could have bitten her tongue the moment she said the word. She saw it all in a flash. He had known nothing, nothing!, simply played on her suspicions of George. Somehow he had perceived that she suspected the other man of wrongdoing and had turned this to his own advantage.

"Smuggling? What can you mean?" His laughter roared up into the tower, sneering back and forth across the rough walls. "When you said that earlier, I thought you were in jest! Dull old George a smuggler? Wherever did you get that notion? It's ludicrous."

"Very well, sir! I know not what game you're playing with me, but I'm leaving, right this minute!"

"No you're not!" He was still laughing, but he had stepped over to the door and was blocking it with outstretched arms, his hands resting negligently on either doorpost.

"Why did you bring me here? You promised me news of George and now you say you have none. This is nonsense!" Despite her nervousness, Daphne found that any fear she might have felt earlier in her eerie surroundings was dissipating.

"I'll tell you news. We're to be wed! Isn't that worth coming to this wreck of a tower to discover?"

"Wed? Me, marry you?" Now it was her laughter that filled the room, echoing down the platform above. "I'll do no such thing!"

"Oh, but you will. I assure you."

"Don't count on it!"

"If you don't, your succor of George, if he needs it, which I doubt, will be the last thing you do, at least in respectable society."

"What?"

"You have been too hasty, Miss Daphne dear. Consider your position."

"My position is that I am stuck in an old tower with you. What difference does that make?"

"What difference? You asked what game I was playing. It is a very obvious one, and very common. It's called catch the heiress, by any means required. One method is to woo the girl and elope to Scotland, another is to win her parents' approval and do the proper thing. And if neither of these works there is always the gentle art of compromise."

"Compromise? I can't imagine us reaching any sort of agreement, not even a compromise. You're wasting your time and mine."

"I speak of the other sort of compromise, darling."

"The other ... ?" She was still unafraid, merely exasperated.

"The kind that involves ruining a young lady's reputation so that she has to marry one in order to hush it up. I speak of compromising your virtue."

Her reaction surprised him. After thinking a moment, as if to consider this possibility from all sides, she exclaimed, "Of course! Why didn't I think of that myself? It would be the very sort of thing that would make George propose, if he thought Emily's honor was at stake."

"What are you talking about?"

"Oh, nothing that's any of your business. I'm not going to marry you no matter what you say, so there."

"Why not?" he asked with a laugh. "I'm tolerably handsome, I'd promise not to get in your way, and there are no other prospects in sight for you. Why not settle for me, Daphy?"

She was irritated by his use of her familiar nickname and snapped back, "I'm not in love with you, that's why! I'm in love with . . ." At that moment she realized the enormity of what she had almost revealed, something she had not put into words even to herself.

"You're in love with George, I suppose! That fool! Forget him, he would bore you to death in no time. I'm a better man than he!"

"You're no such thing! George is ten times the man you are. Why, you aren't even a man, not really, using tricks in this cowardly way to make me do what you want. A real man, a gentleman, would never have stooped so low."

He was stung by her contempt. She moved as if to say more, but a threatening shake of his fist silenced her. "Damn your impudence! I'd intended to just give the appearance of the thing, easy enough to do if you stay in this tower with me for the night. But now I'm sorely tempted to take action. I shall teach you a lesson you'll never forget!"

Now fear engulfed Daphne. He was no longer a

laughable popinjay playing at being a fine London dandy, the great lover. For the first time she felt threatened.

She edged back until she felt the stone step nudging stubbornly against her heel. Desperate, she looked around. There was no way to escape him, no way to go but up. She began to climb the steps, her mind toying with the idea of signaling from the window to summon rescue. But signal with what? To whom? Her common sense had not entirely deserted her, despite her fear, and she knew that this was impossible. She would have to rely on herself to fight off this demon. But she had so few weapons to use, least of all strength! Would her wits be enough to save her?

Moving purposefully, Gascoigne reached the bottom step, when the silence around them was shattered. A shriek pierced the air.

"What the hell?" He stared up, then over his shoulder, trying to discover the source of the noise. The shriek, wherever it had come from, was repeated with even more chilling intensity.

"A ghost!" Daphne gasped. She stopped as if frozen on the stairs, then scurried further up them. Anything, even a ghost, was preferable to Gascoigne.

"Don't be ridiculous!" He snapped this out, but there was a note of uncertainty in his voice for all its sharpness.

"It is, too, a ghost! The monks have come back to deal with you! You're violating sacred ground with your talk of compromise and force!" She was jubilant now, so great was her relief and her certainty.

"There is no such thing about!" he snarled, bounding up the steps after her, ignoring the falling stones loosened by his feet. As he reached the first window slit on the spiral, a rustling caught his attention. Too late, he turned to see that something cold and wet and very large was bearing down on him through the narrow window. With a scream of terror, he tried to fight it off, but in the struggle he lost his balance and fell from the steps to the dirt below.

18.

George had lingered after the departure of the other guests, including his cousin Max, from St. Wilfred's Close. He had apologized for his effrontery four times, proffered the hope that as an old friend of the family he might be forgiven this extravagance, and finally been told by Sir Wilfred to go help Emily direct the restoration of certain potted plants to their normal positions in the conservatory.

"Might as well make yourself useful, George, as long as you're to be about," Sir Wilfred had snorted before turning to his wife to thunder, "I guess I'll have to get used to the sight of him, eh? Wish he'd stop shillyshallying."

George's ears still burned with this, for the comment had been made almost to his face, but he took comfort in knowing that he had responded to his host with a bow of dignity, as he should, one that showed he had not really heard a word. Propriety had been upheld. He failed to realize that he had then sped to the conservatory, almost scampered, so ardent was his desire to see Emily.

"The biggest of the two goes to the far end," she was saying as he entered the glass-enclosed room. Two servants, farm-hands pressed into extraordinary service for the night, grinned and pulled their caps before heaving the larger of the pots up between them. Emily, her back to the door, anxious to get as much cleared away as possible before the hour had advanced any further, was unaware of the new arrival.

"Emily!"

"George!" She swung around and hurried to him, then stopped only a step away, her hands dropped quickly to her sides. A blush spread over her face. "I had thought you left with your cousin, sir," she said though her embarrassment.

"Leave at such an early hour? And before taking my leave of you? Nay, I have dallied as long as I could, hoping for a moment of your time and outliving my welcome and your father's patience."

"Papa? Has he said anything?"

George was now blushing. "Only that I might as well be useful instead of merely standing about."

"Oh, dear, that was too bad of him! To order you about in such a manner!"

"No, no, he was well within his rights. All of the others have left long since. He must find my manners

174

unaccountable. And I could offer no fit excuse."

"Why did you stay?" she asked shyly.

"Why, to talk with you, of course. Aside from the one moment alone with you in the alcove, it seemed scarcely longer than a second!, I have seen little of you this evening. Those dances scarcely count for anything."

"I have longed for your company, too, George."

His blush grew even deeper. "And of course, we must discuss how our little effort has prospered this evening."

"Of course," she agreed, hiding her disappointment. The pair of laborers had returned, offering a diversion.

"Yes, yes, the smaller ones are to be put on the bench. Those four there. And be careful of the flowers on them. You know how concerned her ladyship is that all care be taken. They are quite fragile. It would not do to break them off."

"Lady St. Wilfred would be distraught if such were to occur," George agreed solemnly while the pots were removed. "It was quite a pretty array tonight. Quite pretty."

"Papa insisted that it be so. Daphne had talked of making the ballroom into some sort of tent, and he became very upset. He said his mother had used flowers, and that they were quite good enough. So Daphne had to arrange all of these instead of her sheets." She stifled a yawn.

"You are tired, surely this can wait for morning?"

"Mama is most concerned for the more delicate plants,

that they be in their usual environment. It will take but another moment or two."

"It was good of her to allow her precious flowers to be used. I know that some are very rare."

"She was glad that they made such a lovely display, once Daphne had arranged them."

"Daphy did a very pretty job. I'm surprised that she has left it to you to see that they are returned to their proper places."

"She was tired and went up early," Emily explained quickly.

"I intended no criticism! The words were idle, ill-considered chatter. Please believe me!"

"You're not to worry. I know you too well to take umbrage at anything you say. You would never say anything meant to be slighting. And I did not mean for you to think that I had taken offense!"

"Please don't distress yourself over my too hasty words, dearest Emily!" Impulsively, he reached out and took her hand, pressing it in both of his as if to explain himself with his touch. The laborers returned, and the couple sprang apart.

"The palms should go in the hall," Emily gasped.

"We still be working at moving the smallish ones, miss," the older of the men explained.

"Of course, I did not see, I mean . . . Well, after you have moved the small ferns onto the bench by the north window, you should take the palms to their places in the hall."

"Yus, miss." Being a kindly man, he waited until he

176

had rejoined his companion in the conservatory before he allowed himself a grin.

"About Daphne and Max," George said as soon as they were alone again. "Did you notice if they were getting along well tonight?"

Emily frowned. "They seem to be getting along not at all."

"Are you sure?"

Struck by the anxious expression on his face, Emily refrained from saying what she had noticed, that Daphne had spent much of her time with Gerard Gascoigne in close conversation. In fact, it was with Gascoigne alone that she had shown any inclination to linger. "I may have misunderstood what I saw. Or they may have conversed when I was elsewhere."

"So much depends on it!"

"I noticed that your cousin had small taste for the party after Daphne retired," she said, hoping to please him.

"Yes, he did leave early. But for him to have lost his heart and not have the love returned would be even worse than the present state of affairs. He might never marry!"

Emily's face brightened as a new thought struck her. "I can find out for you what Daphne feels!"

"How?"

"By asking her, of course! Not directly, but it's the sort of thing we would talk about, in any case."

"Then by tomorrow we should know something more?"

"Tomorrow? Why should we wait? I shall go up to her room and see if she is still awake. She may well be, for as tired as she was, I'll venture to guess that she was so full of excitement that she might not have fallen asleep yet."

"Emily! Could you? It would relieve my mind of much concern!"

"Of course I could. You must wait here for me. It will take but a minute."

She hurried through the ballroom and up the stairs, her mind in a turmoil. She could not understand why George was so insistent that his cousin be settled in matrimony, and settled quickly. His determination was new to her and he had failed to confide any of his reasons to her. For anyone else she would have hesitated. But not for George. She was going to help him in any way she could, for she was convinced of the rightness of any action he embarked on, knowing him to be a kind, decent man. And she was too much in love with him to deny him anything she could give so easily.

She opened the door to Daphne's room without knocking, hoping to see if her sister was asleep without disturbing her if she was. Long familiarity and custom made this the natural thing for her to do. To her disappointment, the room was in total darkness, not even a night-light burning on the bedside table, which was odd. The curtains were still flung open, however, and as she stood in the doorway straining her eyes toward the pillow, the clouds broke briefly, and a ray of light streaked across the smooth silk of the bed's coverlet.

Daphne wasn't there.

Calling her sister's name, Emily rushed into the room, heedless of the noise she was making, half expecting to find the girl hidden behind the door in some freakish plan to surprise her. The shadows behind the door were empty. She stopped to look under the bed, peeked into the wardrobe, pushing the dresses aside to explore the corners, even checked behind the dresser. In a panic, she turned to the windows to investigate the drapes.

The curtains held no secrets.

For a moment Emily wanted to laugh. That prankster had fooled her again! She must be about somewhere, expecting just such a visit and laying this trap to tease Emily. That must be it! But then the memory of the time that had passed since she saw Daphne off to bed made her stop and think. Surely the girl couldn't have sat up all this time waiting to spring a joke? It was more than an hour past since she had departed for bed, murmuring an embarrassed apology to their parents about the hour being unfamiliarly late to her. And there, crumbled on her chair, was her costume. She *had* been to her room.

Where could she be?

As if in answer, the clouds thinned again, and in the intermittent moonlight bathing the countryside, Emily could see the path toward the tower's cliff, just visible from the window. And along that path a vague figure flitted, moving in and out of the shadows. It was gone in a minute, hidden by a plantation of pines, but she was sure that someone, she couldn't be sure of whom, was moving toward the tower. It had to be someone from the Close, for the path's only access was on the grounds of the house. It must be her sister.

Emily did not know what was happening, but she did know that if it was at all possible, Daphne must be rescued from this escapade without their parents hearing of it. And the only person who could do that for her was George. She flew down the stairs to find him waiting where she had left him.

"George!"

The urgency in her voice warned him. "What? Bad news?"

"The worst!"

"She will not consider Max?"

"No, no, something horrible! She has run off! Or at least I think that's what has happened."

"What are you saying?"

"She is not in her room. And when I was looking out of the window of it, I saw someone moving up the path from the house to the tower. Only people in our household use that path, George. Who else but Daphne could it have been?"

"My God! What could have caused her to leave?" He stared at the startled expression on Emily's face and hazarded a guess. "Gascoigne? That miserable fortune hunter has somehow lured her away! I suspected him of being of low character, but it never occurred to me that he would stoop to seducing a young, innocent . . ."

"George, you must go after her! Bring her back!"

"What? What about your parents? Have you told your father?"

"No, George. It would crush him if he were to find that she had done something so unforgivable. You must bring her back before anyone knows. There mustn't be a scandal!"

"Now, Emily, I cannot help but feel that your father would be the most suitable individual to deal . . ."

"Think of Max."

"What?"

"Could he marry her if her reputation were lost?"

"Well . . ."

"And it would be, if a word of this is breathed to anyone!"

"Your father would never bruit such a thing about!"

"He would feel honor-bound to tell Max what had happened if he were to offer for her. It would be the death of him. There has never been so much as a hint of impropriety in the family for so long. It's a matter of great pride to him."

"Really, now, Emily, I can't believe that he would be so harsh. She is but an impetuous girl."

"If you don't act now, Max will never be able to marry Daphne!"

She had spoken in a tone of such firmness as he had never heard before. "But I'm still in this dashed costume!"

"Go! The walk way outside the French windows leads straight to the tower's path. Hurry! For my sake! I shall be in my room, waiting for you to return."

"But . . ."

"When I see you bringing her back, I shall creep downstairs and unlock the door for her. Never fear."

"How . . ."

"Now go!"

19.

There didn't seem to be need for much action on Daphne's part. The ghost was behaving quite chivalrously.

Gascoigne had managed, after considerable struggle, to escape the icy embrace of the creature that had flown in through the window and fallen on his head. Discouraged, it had lain at his feet, unmoving, once he had shrugged it off. But its colleagues were not yet finished.

A strange rattling had begun somewhere in the air over their heads, only to end in a shower of pebbles raining down on the unfortunate attacker, its pattern wonderfully localized so that he and only he suffered from their pelting blows. As he stumbled toward the door, trying to escape, another apparition loomed large

183

before him, flying down from the dark shadows surrounding the tower. Retreat was blocked.

Daphne was not at all sure that she liked this maneuver, for the scoundrel had been on the run, after all, and she wanted him gone. As he stumbled back into the tower, beating off the newest attacker with flailing fist that seemed to leave no impression on the creature's body, she crept back up the steps. But there was no need for her to fear for her safety.

The outside attacker seemed content that Gascoigne had been mewed in the tower, for it disdained pursuit. Instead, it continued to hover at the door, nearly a foot between it and solid ground, leaving its companions to continue the work. They did.

Gascoigne suffered another shower from above, this time of frogs, toads and mice, most of which seemed to be dead. He brushed them from his head and shoulders with disgust and dismay, staring helplessly first at the apparition still guarding the door and then at the darkness above him from which his immediate tormentor seemed to originate. Daphne heard some curses, mixed with an occasional prayer, leave his lips and she stifled the impulse to giggle. Whoever the ghosts were, she was beginning to like them.

And it seemed there were more coming. Allies from the dark shadows beyond the tower could be heard approaching in a curious shuffling procession broken frequently by howls and moans. The spirits within the tower groaned their greetings and soon the air reverberated with a cacophony of moans, curses, shrieks, rasping sounds, and metallic clinkings. A veritable army of ghosts had gathered.

Daphne, long past worrying for her own safety, was distracted from her admiration of her rescuers, for so they must be termed, by another outburst from Gascoigne.

"Damn you, you witch, stop them! Stop them!"

"I am not a witch!"

"I can't stand any more of this!" A shower of vile-smelling fluid was now pouring down on him and he crouched near the wall, his arms up to offer his head what protection they could. His fine coat and costume beneath it were well bespattered.

"Well, it must be your fault they have come. I certainly didn't ask them! As if I would know any ghosts in the first place! What do you take me for, Mr. Gascoigne?"

"I give up! I'm sorry for what I tried to do! Just leave off with these torments!" He was almost sobbing now, and Daphne found it in her heart to feel a little sorry for him. She smiled to discover she could still surprise herself with pity for this rogue.

"But you aren't really being hurt, are you? Not really? Now do calm down. Maybe that will stop them."

"Calm down? Are you mad?"

A cackle filled the tower, echoing through it from top to bottom and up again. "Mad! Mad!" a voice seemed to be saying. Daphne was laughing despite herself now.

"I think they are quite nice ghosts," she said. "They haven't hurt me at all."

"You're a witch! It's all your fault!"

One of the approaching spirits seemed to take offense at this insult, for a thunderous explosion shook the night air. For a brief moment a flash of light illuminated the area around the tower. Through the window Daphne spied a nearer ghost, in white, writhing on the ground, and a darker form toiling up the path toward the building.

"Mr. Gascoigne, you haven't even seen any monks coming in and out of windows yet, only a plain white ghost or two. I think you are very poor-spirited to take such a fright when only these very minor spooks have appeared. Now, if I were to see some monks, I should really be afraid!"

"Monks?"

"Well, after all, this was once holy ground. You have defiled sanctified ground with your scheming. I expect the local ghosts will want to purge you."

Before he could answer, the hovering ghost at the door was brushed aside and another white form, this with a battered hat perched where a head ought to be, staggered in, groaning. It was too much for Gascoigne. When he saw that the newest spirit on the scene had moved to one side of the doorway, as if to gain the steps, he bolted. A desperate man, he had seen an opportunity to escape and seized it.

He failed. Before he could reach the freedom of the open door, the groaning ghost had espied his intent, and, infuriated, turned on him. The two figures, locked and intertwined, were on the ground in a confused heap after a few convulsive starts and jerks.

"Naw ye don', villain!" it cried. Whatever it was, it seemed to be on top. "I git ye, I git ye!"

"You're not supposed to 'git' anyone, as you well know. You are supposed to scare them away!" a voice snapped in a penetrating whisper that pierced the darkness. "Let him go!"

"That's not fair! One of the other ghosts forced Mr. Gascoigne back into the tower not ten minutes ago!" Daphne shouted with spirit. "Why should this new one not have some fun?"

"Yes, that was all very well, but that was when I still had some more things to throw down on him. I'm all out of toads and such now."

"But I only naow git him!" the tackling spirit complained.

"You should let him have some fun, too, you know," Daphne said in support.

"Daphy, keep out of this! If he'd arrived on time he would have had all the fun he wanted. Besides, it's my show."

"Well, really! And you haven't even put on any monks!" she complained with a giggle.

"I'll monk you!"

"What is going on here?" a new voice thundered from the doorway, silencing all the ghosts, as well as Daphne.

George had left the Close, his lady love's hand firmly between his shoulder blades and shoving, with a heavy heart. Or so he expressed it to himself.

He could not help but doubt the wisdom of this dramatic intervention on his part into what was after all none of his business, as dear as Emily and her family were to him. Not only was it none of his business, it was most positively another man's. Sir Wilfred St. Wilfred's, to be exact. He should be the man struggling up the cliffpath by uncertain moonlight, not George Wade-Hambledon. Which was not to say that George would not have been willing, more than willing, to accompany him and offer any assistance, if he'd been requested to do so.

If only dear Emily was right. If she was, he was performing an heroic task for her favor, by saving her younger sister from a villain and protecting her family's good name from scandal. It was all quite romantical, seen in that light. But what if she was wrong? What if Sir Wilfred found out about it, anyway? What if he decided to hush up the incident, whatever the incident was, and, keeping his daughter's youth and inexperience in mind, not tell anyone? Or what if Max offered for Daphne despite this terrible lapse from decorum? What if he, George Wade-Hambledon, was on a fool's errand?

And what if he couldn't stop Gascoigne?

Far ahead of him he saw a tottering figure, heretofore invisible in the darkness, suddenly envelop itself in a white, cloudlike mass. Interested, he hastened his step. Then the sound of an explosion, accompanied by a flash of light, broke the night's silence for miles around and he broke into a run. Whatever was afoot, it now sounded dangerous.

He could hear voices calling out to one another as he neared the tower, but could not make out the exact meaning of more than a few scattered words. All activity seemed to have moved inside. Near the door, he stumbled over a long solid object on the ground. In the dim light he could just perceive a musket lying at his feet. So much for the explosion. He prayed under his breath that no one had been injured, even killed, and that this was the last of the firearms he would see that night. At the entrance to the tower, another hazard, a tangle of white, nearly tripped him, but he reached the door safely.

The scene that met his eyes as he stepped over the threshold was a curious one, and he disliked curiosities almost as much as he disliked upstarts who seduced young girls. On the floor at his feet, two men, one still wrapped in the white cloak George now saw was a sheet, were struggling. White Cloak seemed to be on top of the situation, literally and figuratively, if the moans from his opponent were any clue.

And on the steps on the far side of the room, lit by moonlight flowing in through the window immediately above her head, sat Daphne, giggling. A board overhead creaked.

"What is going on here?" No answer. "Well, can't one of you answer me? Daphne? Who are these people on the ground here?"

Daphne caught her breath and swallowed a chuckle. "One of them is Mr. Gascoigne, George. He tricked me into coming here to meet him."

"Then you weren't aware of his plan? You are but an innocent victim?"

"Well, I suppose you could put it that way."

"Whatever possessed you to come out on a night like this to meet such a dastardly scoundrel as Gerard Gascoigne, Daphne? It was the height of folly, as well as being most unbecoming."

"Pooh!" a voice overhead snorted.

"What was that! Who else is here? You, you up there!" Here he shook his fist at the ceiling overhead. "Come down this instant!"

"OOOOHHH!" the voice amended.

"You can't fool me, I heard you. Come down this instant!"

"I think perhaps you should come down," Daphne suggested in a small voice from her perch on the steps.

"And explain yourself, too!" this from George.

There was the sound of grumbling, followed by the creak of the rungs of the ladder. A moment later, another white-sheeted figure appeared on the stairs above Daphne.

"Now, we are going to get to the bottom of this!" George announced with satisfaction. "Daphne, why did you come here, who is this creature on the floor in a sheet? Who is that person on the steps, and what are they doing here? Furthermore . . ."

"MOOOORE!"

They froze. The whisper, ghastly in the darkness, groaned through the still air of the tower, ending in a harsh rasp.

"It's outside! I mean, a real ghost is outside!" the ghost on the steps gasped.

Before they could say anything more, a rustling drew all eyes to the doorway. Standing there, dark against the moonlit landscape, was the figure of a tall man, swaying in the opening. And he wore the robes of a medieval monk!

20.

The only sound in the tower was Gascoigne's labored breathing. Everyone stared at the apparition in the door, waiting for someone else to speak the first word, take the first step. No one did.

"Who are you!" the figure suddenly hissed, pointing with a long, awful hand toward the shivering white form on the steps. That individual, whether flesh or spirit, was unable to do more than chatter back.

"Answer meeee!"

"It is, I mean, he is my brother, Willie St. Wilfred," Daphne said with what courage she could muster.

"And why is he here, mocking me and mine?"

"He is not precisely mocking anyone, Sir Ghost." She moved to a protective stance at the foot of the stairs and turned to the dark figure in the door as if in defiance.

"Whyyyy?"

"Yes, why?" George asked, shaken from his fearful silence by an overpowering curiosity.

Willie still could not answer and they turned back to Daphne. "I think, at least I believe, that he has been trying to scare people away from the tower!"

"Then he has failed," the monk laughed sardonically.

"There do seem to be quite a number of people here tonight, Sir Ghost," she agreed.

"But that does not answer the question. What mischief has been afoot here?" George asked, his tone repressive and heavy with disapproval. "What has Willie been up to?"

Daphne, realizing that it would take more than a monkish ghost to repress George, sighed and answered. "I would guess that he has been studying the stars from the top of the tower."

George looked horrified. "What? Has he taken up astrology again? His parents have expressly forbidden it!"

"Not astrology! Astronomy!" Daphne protested.

"There is no difference!"

Defense came from an unexpected corner. "A real difference," the ghost hissed. This hasty comment drew a suspicious look from the girl.

"I found what must have been a telescope case hidden up there," she continued. "At first I thought it had something to do with smuggling and I couldn't get it open for a proper look, so I didn't realize what it was."

"Smuggling? What foolishness is this? There is no smuggling hereabouts!" George protested.

"Yes, well, I thought that maybe . . ."

"Whatever put that into your head?"

"Youuuuu!"

"I?" He was aghast.

Daphne, hesitated, wishing the ghost had kept his mouth shut, then tried to explain. "You have behaved so strangely whenever the tower was mentioned, that I thought you must have some, well, some guilty secret connected with it, and I tried to find out what it was, and the only thing I could think of was smuggling, and I was so very worried!"

"Smuggling?" The ghost on the stairs had finally found its tongue. "George, a smuggler? You silly widgeon! Of all the fiddle-faddle, to convince yourself of such a preposterous notion! Why, why!" Willie, at a loss for words, ended with a whoop of laughter.

"Don't you dare laugh at me, Willie St. Wilfred! You are just as foolish, running around pretending to be a ghost, and getting old Jed here involved with you, too! You should be ashamed of yourself, on his account if not your own!"

"There, there, now, quiet yourselves! There is to be no arguing. Most unbecoming!" George commanded fussily, perhaps irritated that his thunder had been stolen. "This is nothing but foolishness. Daphne, how could you believe such a thing of me I cannot understand!"

"Eeeasileeee!"

The ghastly hiss brought them back to the reality of their situation, for in the heat of the moment they had forgotten that they were the prisoners of the monkish spirit.

Satisfied that he had their attention, the ghost continued. "George Wade-Hambledon, you have been as foolish as they!"

"What? Well, I must say, you have a nerve . . ."

"Silence!"

George obeyed.

"You will take this Gascoigne back to Forbisher Grange this night."

George stood on his dignity. "That is all very well to suggest, but I must get Miss Daphne, and now her brother, back to the Close. Emmy, I mean, her sister, is waiting up to let her in without anyone finding out about this escapade, and I promised her I would get the girl home."

"I do not suggest. I command!"

George was not abashed. "And how dare you call me foolish!" he continued, as if he had not heard the interruption.

"You are foolish because you have had happiness in your grasp and have failed to take it!"

"I say . . ."

"You have all come here seeking! The lad, Willie, sought knowledge. The old man sought a reason for living in his service to his young master. Gascoigne," here he kicked the abject figure at his feet, "Gascoigne sought a fortune. Daphne sought the truth."

There was a long silence as they waited to hear what he would say about George. Aware that all eyes were on him, that worthy turned to the ghost and demanded, "And I? What of me?"

"You came to win a lady's favor, even if it meant

risking your dignity and betraying your conscience."

"It was a small enough thing to do for an old friend, a mere trifling favor, the least I could do . . ." George sputtered.

"You sought to win her favor in love. You had that love long ago. Now you must seek her hand in marriage!"

"Of all the dashed impertinence!"

"Do shush up, George! He's right, you know! Just listen to what he has to say and then do it!" Daphne ordered.

But George, his wits sharpened, perhaps by embarrassment, turned back to the ghost. "I say, just who are you, anyway? Is this some sort of practical joke?"

"You will take this scoundrel back to Forbisher Grange this night, before the tale is known throughout the countryside. And tomorrow . . ."

Despite himself, George was listening. "Yes?"

"Tomorrow you will ask, nay, beg for the hand of Miss St. Wilfred in marriage!"

"But I can't do that."

"You had damned well better!" the ghost said with exasperation. "You do want to, don't you?"

"Well, yes, of course, I always have, but . . ."

"Max! It's Max! How could you do such a thing to us!" Daphne cried out, torn between laughter and anger.

"Max!" George gasped with dismay.

"Blast it, Daphy, why couldn't you have held your tongue?" the monk asked with disgust.

"You've been listening outside all along!" she accused.

"Of course."

"What? How?" his cousin asked.

The ghost sighed, removing his concealing cloak.

"I guessed something was afoot when Gascoigne left early and Daphy disappeared soon after. So I went after Gascoigne."

"What a complete hand you are, sir!" Willie exclaimed, much impressed.

"I must say, Max, that this sort of jape is beneath your touch. Shocking!" George complained.

"Silence!"

They obeyed.

"Am I not the head of our family?"

"Yes," George answered meekly.

"And don't you owe me every sign of respect and obedience?"

"Well, yes."

"I should hope you'd say yes. You keep talking about if often enough."

"But . . ."

"I'd hate to discover that you've been lying to me all these years, acting the hypocrite. Now, you will follow my orders to the letter!"

"I am more than willing to take this ill-bred ruffian back to where he belongs, provided you will see to Daphne's safety."

"Of course."

"As to the rest . . ."

"If you don't marry Emily, I shall disown you!" he snapped. "What a dimwit you are. I'm insisting on it for your own good, you know. You're hopelessly in love with her."

"It is my business."

"And you are handling it quite badly. Do as you're told, George," Max answered with an exasperated sigh.

"There is something that you are not aware of that may impede the pursuit of a course that would follow the dictates of my heart!" George explained with ponderous dignity.

Daphne sat up. "I knew it!"

"If you're not a smuggler, George, what are you?" Willie chimed in.

"Surely you can't have a dishonorable past?" Daphne giggled.

"It is nothing in the least dishonorable!" he thundered.

Max studied the other man's discomfort for a moment and then said, "Leave him in peace, you two madcaps!"

George gathered what shreds of his dignity were left him and bowed to the 'monk.' "I shall leave at once with this rogue, cousin. As to the rest of your suggestion, we shall have to discuss the matter, between the two of us, in a more private and dignified setting!" He reached down and grabbed Gascoigne by the collar, pulling him protesting to his feet. No one else said a word until he had left the tower with his charge dragging beside him.

"Does that mean he won't marry Emily?" Daphne asked in a small voice.

Willie scowled at the empty door. "Probably. And she will do nothing but mope, I dare say."

"How could you be so cruel?"

"I'm not cruel! She's been pining away for him these months past, though I can't fathom why," he answered crossly. "Now it will be even worse."

"Really, now! You should have more sympathy."

There was a long, brittle silence. "What will happen?" the girl finally asked.

"I shall do what I can for your sister, Daphy," Max said in a weary voice. "But I fear that George will prove stubborn. When he takes on one of these moods, he is very nearly immovable."

Emily's brother and sister heard this with respectful silence, Willie shaken out of his flippant mood.

"Poor Emmy!" he murmured.

"She will be heartbroken! Crushed!" Daphne said as the tears began to fall down her cheeks.

"Whether or not this will be the case, it is late now. I must get you two safely home. Emily must be quite frantic with worry by now."

"How can I face her?" Daphne wailed.

"I know not. But it will all be settled in the morning. Come away, both of you."

Climbing down from his perch, Willie turned to old Jed's silent form. "Well, our game is up, old boy. Thanks for all you've done these months past. I only hope my father will not deal too harshly with you."

The old man shook with silent laughter. "I do it all again fer ye, Master Willie."

"Even to stumbling and setting off a musket, perhaps to fill some innocent bystander with shot?" Max asked.

"Even ter that!"

200

Willie shook the old man's hand. "And I thank you for it!"

"But now it's time to be off," Max said firmly. "I'll do what I can on your account, too. Although a worse pair of scamps I have never laid eyes on!"

"Must Father be told of the telescope?" Willie asked wistfully.

"I fear so. These clandestine activities are hardly proper. You must stop them."

Wearily, the party found its way out into the bright moonlight. "Just as the sky is finally clearing, I have to leave," Willie grumbled, but no one paid him any heed. Daphne, too tired to consider her action, took Max's hand as if it was quite the most natural thing in the world, and no one, least of all Max, saw fit to comment.

As they reached the grounds of the Close, Daphne found herself near tears with exhaustion and pity. "Poor Emmy! Not even you can fix this one, Max!"

21.

Daphne had decided not to tell Emily anything about the night's events except to assure her that all was well and that Gascoigne, who had lured her away under false pretenses, had received his just desserts. Willie, whom she had sworn to silence, was too sleepy to add anything anyway.

The next morning, when a somber George arrived with his cousin in attendance, the older girl was unprepared for what happened. First, George and Max were closeted with Sir Wilfred and Lady St. Wilfred in the library for nearly an hour, then George came and sought her out, suggesting that they visit the unoccupied music room. Emily, trembling, complied, casting a beseeching glance over her shoulder at her sister as she was led away.

Daphne, not sure if George's solemnity portended ill or well for her sister, waylaid Max as soon as he set foot out of the library.

"Well, did it work? Did you fix things up?"

"I had a dashed time of it, but your father has agreed not to punish Willie for his escapades with the telescope! In fact, he was feeling decidedly sympathetic just a moment ago."

"Willie? Escapades? What do I care of that? I'm concerned about Emily. Will they marry?"

He turned to her, a serious look on his face. "I don't know."

"How can you say that? Hasn't Papa given his permission for them to wed? Why else would George be talking to her now, alone?"

"Your Papa gave only provisional approval for the engagement."

"Provisional?"

"It is up to Emily to decide for herself."

"Then all is well!" she declared happily. "We know what her answer will be."

He grimaced wryly as he heard these words. "George has managed to surprise us all, Daphy. Nothing is assured,"

"What?" Shocked, she cast her mind over the possible misdemeanors that George could have committed, misdemeanors sufficient to turn Emily from him. In her innocence, there were few. "He must have done something shocking!"

"Not shocking, only surprising. And unconventional, if you can imagine such a thing of George. Emily may not be prepared to accept it," Max said absently, his eyes straying to the music room door.

"But he must have done some heinous crime for Emily not to want to marry him."

"Done?" He was laughing at her now. "You little goose, it isn't what he's done, it's what he wants to do!"

"But, still? What in the world is it? Do tell me!"

He silenced her with a wave of his hand, for the couple were coming from the music room.

At first Daphne could see only the tears in her sister's eyes, and her heart sank. Then she noticed that Emily was clinging to George's hand with the tenacity of a limpet, and hope rose in her breast.

"Emily?" she asked shyly. "Has all gone well?"

"It's wonderful! Everything is wonderful!" her sister gasped through her tears.

"Thank goodness! But why are you crying?"

"I'm so happy!"

"What?"

"Congratulations, George! You are a very fortunate man," Max said. "I knew that Emily would see things your way."

"I know I am extremely fortunate, an extremely fortunate man," George said with greater simplicity than usual.

"I wish you both all the happiness in the world," Daphne added.

Willie, who had come running in from the garden in time to hear the announcement, chimed in. "It's about time."

"We must inform Sir Wilfred and Lady St. Wilfred of Emily's decision," George said with a return to his pomposity.

As they turned toward the library, where the parents awaited their daughter's decision, Daphne howled a protest and grabbed each by the arm. "Wait a minute! I don't understand! What is this dreadful secret of George's, that he thought so bad you might not marry him?"

"Dreadful secret? What can you mean?" Emily protested.

"Well, if he isn't a smuggler, what is he?"

"Smuggler?" It took some minutes to soothe the dismay Emily felt, and to explain to her her younger sister's wild flight of fancy, including how it led to the adventure in the tower.

"My George could never have a guilty secret!" she stated firmly, reclaiming her fiancé's hand as she did so. "I know!"

"Yes, that is all very fine, but why did he act like a cat on hot bricks every time I mentioned the tower?" Daphne wailed.

"Did I do that?" George seemed surprised.

"Yes, you did!"

"But I can't imagine how I could have done so," he said with perplexity. His brow furrowed as he puzzled over this. "There was no reason."

"Perhaps I can help," Max offered.

"Please do!" Daphne begged, tartly. "I shall die if someone doesn't tell me soon!"

"It would never do to let that happen!"

He held their attention for a long, silent moment, then relented with a grin. "Was it the tower you mentioned to George, or the church attached to it that made him so uncomfortable?"

"The tower! At least . . ." Her voice trailed off as she thought hard, but her sister had reached the answer for her.

"The *church* tower. You spoke to him of the church!"

"Well, yes, I did. And the ruins of the church, too."

"Whatever for?" Emily wanted to know.

"Well, if you must ask, I was hinting around about a wedding for the two of you. I could not understand why he hadn't proposed yet, and I wanted to find out. He spoke so strangely of marriages and weddings that it only confused things more. He seemed quite happy enough with the idea of getting married, and urged me to consider it. But he said not a word about marrying you, and when I said something about how romantic churches are, just the thing to make you think of weddings, he suddenly puckered up. Was it the idea of marriage that disturbed him?"

At this point, Max and Emily, and finally even George, were laughing helplessly.

"This isn't fair!" Daphne protested.

"I should say not!" Willie agreed.

"It was your talk of the Church that disturbed George," Emily said through her laughter. "Not the tower or weddings."

"It was in the direction of the Church that his guilt lay!" Max added.

"It was not precisely a guilty conscience that affected

my actions, Daphy, for I have done nothing repre-hensible, no matter what Max may hint. Far from it."

Max snorted.

"You have merely stirred up a hornets' nest with your exaggerated sense of propriety and convention. If only you had spoken to me first, before going off on some hare-brained scheme of your own to make everything right!"

"George behaved as he thought proper, m'lord," Emily protested, quick to defend her love. "He had only the best intentions for everyone in everything he did."

"But what is it all about?" complained the younger St. Wilfreds.

The three turned from their engrossing squabble to face this wailing chorus. "What?" George replied. "Haven't we made it all clear enough?"

"No!"

"Far from it!"

The brother and sister had spoken at the same time, both voices filled with indignation.

Emily smiled and held up her hand for silence. "George wishes to enter the clergy," she said with pride.

Her siblings looked at her with disgust.

"Is that all?" Willie asked as he sat down on the window seat with a thud. "Fustian!"

"Piffle!" his sister agreed.

"But Daphy, surely you must see what a serious step it is for him to take!" Emily said.

"Fuss and bother."

"It is not at all the thing for the heir to a marquisate

and other honors to become a clergyman," George lectured with all his dignity. "I could not in good conscience take such a step without there being some hope that my cousin would one day have a son of his own, thus leaving me free to follow my vocation without the dread of being called upon to assume the burden of family duties related to the title."

"Of all the muttonheaded things to do!" Willie said, but his oldest sister shushed him before he could go any further.

"Wasn't there a bishop who was also an earl?" Daphne asked. "I believe Papa has a book written by him. If he could do it, why couldn't you, George?"

"Because, well . . ." For once, George was at a loss for words.

"Because the Bishop-Earl of Bristol did very little ministering to his flock, Daphne," Max explained. "He went off to live in Italy, study architecture and collect art objects, as would any other wealthy nobleman of similar tastes."

"George wants to take an active role among the poor and needy," Emily added, as if this made it all clear. "And I shall help him!"

"I could hardly ask my dearest Emily to share my life if I had no certainty of what that life was to consist, could I?" George asked with a resumption of his air of perfect reasonableness.

"If you loved her, why didn't you . . ."

Max cut in. "That will do, Daphy. It's high time your parents were told of Emily's decision."

"We have dallied too long!" George exclaimed.

"Emily?" He took her hand as they moved down the hall to the library, and Daphne saw that her sister was pink with pleasure.

"She looks very happy," she said in a small voice.

"They both do," Max agreed.

22.

After George and Emily had disappeared into the library, Willie turned the conversation to his predicament.

"I think I shall go fetch my telescope home now," he announced. "I shall have to show it to Papa sooner or later."

"You needn't worry about that," Max assured him. "He's almost reconciled to your interest in astronomy."

"He is? Then I wager it was your doing, sir!"

"Well, at least I convinced him it is now a science and not black magic or witchcraft. That put him in a better frame of mind toward it." Suddenly Max grinned. "Although an account of your hauntings gave him reason to pause!"

"It was rather jolly to be able to try out *all* my

tricks on someone, you know," Willie said with simple pride. "Mr. Gascoigne was our first opportunity. We had worked so hard rigging them up that it was a bit of a letdown when no one came about the place!"

"You have my utmost sympathy!" his sister snapped.

"It is nice to have your work appreciated," Max soothed.

"And it was all your fault that I was nearly caught out, before I had a chance to rescue you, Daphy!" the boy retorted, ignoring the tactful intervention.

"Mine? What did I do?"

"All those sheets for the ball! The housemaids couldn't find the old ones because I had taken them to use at the tower. I was never so relieved as when I heard Papa intervene and order everything taken back to the linen closet!"

"You silly gudgeon! Mama would have noticed they were gone eventually. She makes an inventory of the linen every spring and fall!"

"Well, I would have thought of something by then."

"No, you would not have! You didn't even know she did such things, did you? Just like a silly boy!"

"Just how did you arrange for such a variety of ghosts, sheets aside?" Max interrupted.

"Oh, that was nothing!" the boy said with a show of modesty. "It was a simple matter of ropes and hooks, you see. We arranged all the sheets and lines before we went to the tower, then bundled them up so that I could carry them with me whenever I was using the telescope. It was all quite light and easy to carry. We also trapped rain water when we could to dampen some of the sheets so that they would be suitably chilling to anyone who came close enough to touch."

"And Jed?"

"He waited outside, done up in sheets, standing guard of the tower. He was late last night, I fear, otherwise things might have been settled more quickly."

"Emily must have seen him from Daphne's window. It was because of that that she sent George, so don't judge too harshly," Max mused. "On the other hand, if he'd been at his post, he might have scared off Gascoigne!"

"And Daphy!" the boy agreed with a grin.

"But what of the gun?"

Willie hung his head. "I didn't know he had been carrying his blunderbuss with him. He always kept it out of my sight. I shouldn't have let that happen."

"It was very dangerous," Daphne scolded. "He wouldn't have done it if you hadn't put him up to this guarding stunt!"

"Luckily, his wound was a mere bruise when he fell down last night and not a load of shot."

"Oh, I know, sir," Willie said with a hangdog air.

"I would have thought it rather difficult to make your ghosts travel in and out of windows, if I hadn't seen it with my own eyes," Max said with an encouraging grin.

The boy brightened. "Not at all! We simply let out a line from the top window, and pulled everything in through a bottom one. It was even easier to reverse the action to get the ghost to move up outside the tower. It took practice, but I've enough skill to aim a wet sheet through the window on top of someone's head. Pretty neat, what?"

"If you needed to, what with that old man capering outside the tower!"

"It's best to be prepared."

"And the shower of vermin?"

"Oh, that! That was a new idea. I got if from Daphy."

His sister looked indignant when she heard this. "From me?"

"You did throw mice at Emily that day she fainted, didn't you? It seemed a good notion to me at the time, so I appropriated it for my own purposes."

"Very clever of both of you!" Max said before Daphne could protest further.

"Thank you, sir," Willie answered.

"If you are so clever, Willie, why did you leave your telescope lying about? I found its hiding-place, easily enough. Anyone could have done so, and even stolen it from you. Or taken it to Papa! Then your goose would have been cooked."

"It's a delicate instrument and not to be jostled by carrying it about, Daphy. You did it no good with your rough handling that day, I can assure you."

But Daphne wasn't having any of that, and merely pressed her attack. "I never would have found it if it hadn't been for your ladder being out. That was another silly mistake."

"Dash it all, Daphy, I can't think of everything, can I? I'd made some particularly interesting observations the night before, and was more concerned with writing up my notes than with bothering about an old ladder."

"It nearly caught you out! All that planning gone for nothing because you left your ladder out!"

"Only a Nosey Parker like you would poke into . . ."

"And anyone else who happened to notice that the tower's steps had been repaired. I suppose you got your accomplice Jed to do that for you? He used to be handy with stone and mortar, I recollect."

"Accomplice?" Willie seemed ready to burst.

"No, now, calm down!" They had each opened their mouths as if to protest further when Max added, "Silence! Daphne, you should be thankful that your brother was there to rescue you from Gascoigne."

"You would have done so if he hadn't!"

"I might have missed my way following him from the Close. It was a very dark night. Then it would have all been left in Willie's capable hands."

Willie preened himself.

"There was George, too!"

"By the merest chance." He looked at her steadily, and after a moment she lowered her eyes.

"You ghosts were really quite good, Willie. Thank you for rushing them to my aide," she murmured after another pause.

"Not at all, not at all," he murmured, abashed.

"After all, it was very satisfying to Willie to have an audience for them all!" Max laughed.

The brother and sister grinned sheepishly at him, then at one another.

"The look on George's face was jolly good when he saw the ghosts!" Daphne said with sudden enthusiasm.

"Your spirits were positively horrific," Max added.

"But your arrival as a dark monk topped them all," Willie said generously.

"It was lucky I had a black cloak with me. It was just the thing especially after Daphne asked for a monk so particularly."

"It fooled all of us!"

Max cuffed Willie's head gently. "Willie, your father has promised to consider helping you set up some sort of observatory nearer home. Perhaps if you were to show him the telescope, let him use it some evening, he will better appreciate your interest in the stars."

"Yes, sir!"

Despite his enthusiasm, Willie had begun shifting his weight from foot to foot in a manner familiar to anyone who had any acquaintanceship with young boys. Max grinned.

"You're anxious to get your telescope. Run along now."

"Yes, sir!" His thin face eager and alive, he was out the door in an instant.

Now that they were alone, Max turned to Daphne and smiled. "Shall we go sit in the garden, Daphy?"

"By all means. And perhaps you can explain to me why in the world George couldn't have simply told everybody he wanted to be a clergyman, like any sensible person would. I cannot understand. It would have saved us all this bother."

"What is sensible to you and me would not do for George. Emily is right. He thought he was doing the right thing."

"But . . ."

"He would have turned his back on his vocation, which I perceive to be a very real one, if he thought I was never to marry and get an heir of my own. He would have felt it was his duty."

They had reached the garden bench and Daphne arranged her skirts neatly over the stone surface while Max made himself comfortable beside her.

"It all began here," he said softly.

"What? Yes, we did meet here," she answered, suddenly shy. "I was tossing mice through the window." She was giggling at the memory, her exasperation, even her shyness, forgotten.

"Well do I remember." After a moment of silence he added, "Do you really regret all that has passed since then? None of it would have happened if George had done the sensible thing."

The girl blushed and avoided his gaze. "Of course not. We had great fun, you and I, I mean, the four of us. And I have had an adventure. And George has proved himself worthy of Emily."

This surprised him. "How so?"

"You said it yourself. He was willing to fib, for her sake, to cover up for me when they thought I had run off. That was a truly noble sacrifice of principles for him to make!"

Max grinned. "So it was."

He waited a moment, then ventured, "You will have your Season now without any worries about Emily."

"Yes, I suppose so."

"You'll enjoy it all tremendously, I'm sure. You're bound to be a success."

"Will you be there?"

He looked at her thoughtfully, solemn despite the eagerness in her voice. "I'm not sure."

Her face fell.

"There will be others to dance the waltz with you at Almack's."

"But none like you. You're my friend!"

"Yes, but . . ."

"I bet you'd dance the waltz with me even if none of the Patronesses said we could."

"Surely not!"

"Oh, yes."

"We'd be outcasts!"

For a moment they smiled at each other, then started laughing. Then Max reached his hand in his pocket, a look of uncertainty on his face.

"What is it?" she asked.

"I had gotten it ready, but then I thought I should wait, until after London."

"Wait! Oh, don't do that."

"You'll understand when you see it." He handed her the box.

It was small and wrapped in gay-colored tissue paper, and when she had ripped off its yellow covering, she saw that it was laced with tiny holes. Cautiously, she opened the lid and peeked inside.

"Oh!" She was so startled by what she saw that she nearly dropped the box and its contents.

"Max!" She sounded bewildered and indignant. "What's this all about? Are you making fun of me?"

"You're supposed to faint into my arms, Daphy!"

"Faint? But it's only a mouse!" Reaching into the box, she drew out a small, wiggly bit of fur. "Where did you find it?"

"In the stables. I didn't precisely capture it myself. I left that to the head groom and his lads."

"But why give it to me?"

"I've already told you. You're supposed to faint!"

Her eyes widened and she felt herself growing pink. "But I'm not afraid of mice!" she mumbled.

"It worked for George and Emily."

"Very slowly."

"Must I also enter the clergy to attract your favor? I pray not, for I fear I've no vocation for that sort of thing."

She was scarlet now, but glancing up at him shyly from beneath her lashes. "I could pretend to faint."

"Thank you. But on second thought, you're right. It took George and Emily a dashed long time to get things settled. We might do better if you stay awake instead."

She smiled and arranged her skirts demurely about her ankles. "Very well."

"Daphne St. Wilfred, will you marry me?"

"Yes."

He grinned and grabbed her. "Thank God!" They clung to one another for a moment, Daphne experiencing her first kiss and finding she liked it, and then Max started to laugh.

"What's so funny?" she asked indignantly, shoving him away from her. "Have I done something wrong?"

"Wrong? Oh, no my love, never that!" He kissed her

again, proving his point to both their satisfactions.

After a moment she murmured, "Why were you laughing?"

"I was thinking how pleased your father would be."

"He does like you."

"More than that."

"Hmm?"

"It means he won't have to go up to London to shoot you off! I warned you earlier that it might be a good idea to wait until after you had started your Season. Now you won't have one, not really."

"Yes, I shall! Any time I feel like it. As a married lady. You will let me, won't you?"

"Yes, darling, I shall."

"Promise?"

"With all my heart."

THRILLS * CHILLS * MYSTERY
from FAWCETT BOOKS

THE GREEN RIPPER by John D. MacDonald	14340	$2.50
MURDER IN THREE ACTS by Agatha Christie	03188	$1.75
NINE O'CLOCK TIDE by Mignon G. Eberhart	04527	$1.95
DEAD LOW TIDE by John D. MacDonald	14166	$1.75
DEATH OF AN EXPERT WITNESS by P. D. James	04301	$1.95
PRELUDE TO TERROR by Helen MacInnes	24034	$2.50
AN UNSUITABLE JOB FOR A WOMAN by P. D. James	00297	$1.75
GIDEON'S SPORT by J. J. Marric	04405	$1.75
THURSDAY THE RABBI WALKED OUT by Harry Kemelman	24070	$2.25
ASSIGNMENT SILVER SCORPION by Edward S. Aarons	14294	$1.95

This offer expires 1 July 81   8400-2

CURRENT BESTSELLERS
from POPULAR LIBRARY

A NEW DECADE OF CREST BESTSELLERS

RESTORING THE AMERICAN DREAM		
Robert J. Ringer	24314	$2.95
THE LAST ENCHANTMENT *Mary Stewart*	24207	$2.95
THE SPRING OF THE TIGER *Victoria Holt*	24297	$2.75
THE POWER EATERS *Diana Davenport*	24287	$2.75
A WALK ACROSS AMERICA *Peter Jenkins*	24277	$2.75
SUNFLOWER *Marilyn Sharp*	24269	$2.50
BRIGHT FLOWS THE RIVER		
Taylor Caldwell	24149	$2.95
CENTENNIAL *James A. Michener*	23494	$2.95
CHESAPEAKE *James A. Michener*	24163	$3.95
THE COUP *John Updike*	24259	$2.95
DRESS GRAY *Lucian K. Truscott IV.*	24158	$2.75
THE GLASS FLAME *Phyllis A. Whitney*	24130	$2.25
PRELUDE TO TERROR *Helen MacInnes*	24034	$2.50
SHOSHA *Isaac Bashevis Singer*	23997	$2.50
THE STORRINGTON PAPERS		
Dorothy Eden	24239	$2.50
THURSDAY THE RABBI WALKED OUT		
Harry Kemelman	24070	$2.25

Buy them at your local bookstore or use this handy coupon for ordering.

COLUMBIA BOOK SERVICE (a CBS Publications Co.)
32275 Mally Road, P.O. Box FB, Madison Heights, MI 48071

Please send me the books I have checked above. Orders for less than 5 books must include 75¢ for the first book and 25¢ for each additional book to cover postage and handling. Orders for 5 books or more postage is FREE. Send check or money order only.

Cost $_____   Name _____

Sales tax*_____   Address _____

Postage_____   City _____

Total $_____   State _____ Zip _____

* *The government requires us to collect sales tax in all states except AK, DE, MT, NH and OR.*
